KILLING QUICK

KILLING
QUICK

DWIGHT M. EDWARDS

iUniverse, Inc.

New York   Bloomington

Killing Quick

iUniverse books may be ordered through booksellers or by contacting:

iUniverse
1663 Liberty Drive
Bloomington, IN 47403
www.iuniverse.com
1-800-Authors (1-800-288-4677)

ISBN: 978-1-4401-6987-8 (sc)
ISBN: 978-1-4401-6988-5 (ebk)

Printed in the United States of America

iUniverse rev. date: 09/15/2009

CHAPTER

Dana Travis knew the minute he got home that someone had been there. Nothing obvious, just subtle signs that only a fastidious person like he would spot; particles of dirt resting against the base of a flowerpot, a shirt hanging carelessly off a hanger in the closet, furniture casters that didn't match up with carpet indentations—all telltale signs that furniture had been moved. He grabbed a cold beer from the refrigerator and went down the hall to his study.

There he found more evidence of tampering. Reference books had been put back on the shelf in the wrong order, an accounting ledger was missing, and his desk drawer showed faint scratch marks from being jimmied. Travis propped his stocky legs on the desk and took another sip of beer. *They have no idea what they're looking for. By the time they figure it out, it'll be too late.* He thumbed through his Rolodex until he found the number. For a split moment he considered throwing in the towel and getting out of town while he still could, but greed won out. *It's just a matter of time before he pays—just a matter of time.* What Travis didn't know was that he didn't have any left.

The Legends Hotel lounge was adorned in burgundy and teal accented by brass handrails and trim with wine-colored Berber carpet covering all but 900 square feet of the floor occupied by the white Wurlitzer.

Several people were listening to the latest pianist playing *"Ribbon in the Sky."* The crowd gave her a warm and appreciative applause as she returned to the bar and her waiting husband. The white laminated piano seat sat empty, glowing like a radiant throne beckoning another challenger to come forth, but no one did.

Anna Mateo sat at a nearby table cradling a margarita while staring at the blank laptop screen. This was her second notebook and third hard drive crash in the last six months and it brought to mind the conversation she'd had with her boss a few days ago in the office. "How do you expect me to write the news if you don't give me what I need to do my job?"

'I don't like the situation any more than you, but money is tight right now," he said. She reminded him that this was an election year and the paper had yet to hire a political analyst. Her boss shrugged his shoulders in despair. "We'll have to use existing staff to fill the gaps until we're able to hire more reporters."

"Filling the gaps" translated into Anna getting stuck with additional assignments and longer work hours. Tonight she was covering the state elections. She closed the defective computer and tossed it onto the seat beside her. A reporter from the Post entered the room and waved to her as she muscled her way through the crowed to get to the bar. On any other night the women would have been hanging out together, but this was no ordinary night. This was Primary Tuesday and competing reporters didn't have time to be friends. People had been converging on the lounge since early afternoon. Now that the polls were closed, the room was crowded with onlookers watching the plasma screen. Crowds this large rarely showed up for a presidential election, much less a primary.

Channel 5 began announcing their exit poll results. The race for Governor was going down to the wire. The Democratic incumbent was involved in a fight of his life against his upstart opponent, and the winner wouldn't be known for hours. An even greater shocker was the race for the Republican U.S. Senate nomination. A former U.S. senator and heavy favorite to win the party nomination and general election, was going down in heavy defeat to the Mayor of Evergreen, Victor Alpine. Alpine had been behind in the polls just two weeks ago and now political analysts were projecting he would capture the nomination with fifty-six percent of the vote. Everyone in the room was stunned. Alpine had accomplished something no other politician ever had against this particular opponent; he'd won. There was a whirlwind of cellular activity as reporters scrambled to place calls to their counterparts at Alpine's election headquarters in Evergreen. Every newspaper, radio talk show host, and television news commentator would be scrambling trying to reach Alpine's campaign manager and publicist, Desmond Shaw. Anna could imagine the headline in tomorrow's paper: *Political Neophyte Upsets Underwood!*

Victor Alpine already had quite a track record. He had transformed the second-rate city of Evergreen into a first class economically vital metropolis of 300,000 with the best city services in the state and a revolutionary transit system that had garnered national attention. His accomplishments were nothing less than miraculous, considering he had only been mayor for eight years. Despite all his success, charisma, and popularity, Alpine faced two enormous political liabilities: his age and lack of political experience, either of which should have derailed his candidacy for senator. But here he was still standing. He had proven to be an adept politician who defied the odds.

As much as she was dying to get an interview, Anna knew it wouldn't happen. The only media people allowed access to Victor Alpine were A-team reporters and Anna was so far down the alphabet food chain she knew they'd have to invent a new letter for her. It was just as well because she didn't have the time. She had other political races to cover along with the weekly column she was supposed to have ready by morning. She left the unfinished drink on the table and started to leave.

The bartender caught her attention. "Anna, there's a telephone call for you." He tossed her the cordless phone.

"Hello?" she said.

"Are you Anna Mateo?"

"Yes."

"My name is Dana Travis. I need to talk—"

"How did you find me?"

"Your newspaper told me where you were. I apologize for interrupting you, but I've got to talk to you tonight as soon as possible. I have some information you'll find very interesting."

She raised an eyebrow skeptically. "What kind of information?"

"About Victor Alpine."

"What about him?"

"I have Information that will kill him politically."

She could hear the tension in his voice, but she was irritated and in a hurry. "What is it?"

He paused, but she could hear erratic breathing through the ear pierce. "A conspiracy of sorts."

"Excuse me, Mr. Travis, I don't want to be rude, but can we cut to the chase? I was on my way out when you called."

There was a moment of uncomfortable silence. "What would you say if I told you Victor Alpine knows what happened to Eva Ward?"

Anna froze, almost dropping the phone as she sat down. *Eva…it wasn't possible.* The glimmer of hope and exhilaration quickly gave way to common sense. *Oh great, another headline hunter looking for his fifteen minutes of fame.* All kinds of nuts flooded newsroom switchboards with ridiculous stories following elections. Usually they were pitiful losers who couldn't accept the fact that their candidate had been defeated.

The stories were almost always untrue or imagined accounts of grand conspiracies, adulterous affairs, or corruption. Usually the only truth they revealed was the deep-seated hatred and insecurity of the accuser. But this loser had done some homework. She didn't know what made her angrier; the fact that he was trying to manipulate her loss to his advantage or that he had piqued her interest.

"Are you still there?" he asked.

"Yes. Look, I don't have time to talk to you right now. If you have some information give it to the police, not me."

"I don't trust the police or anyone else for that matter. The only reason I'm talking to you is that I know you were friends with Eva Ward. She's the reason you moved to Washington."

Anna bristled. "How do you know that?"

"It was in one our files."

She didn't like where this was going. "What file?"

"In a corporate vault in San Diego." Clearing his throat, he continued. "I know this must seem strange to you, but I can explain everything when we meet."

In spite of her instinct to hang up the phone, she couldn't. "I'm not meeting you unless you give me something concrete."

"I've already said too much."

Anna rolled her eyes. *This guy has seen too many B-movies.* "Mr. Travis or whatever your real name is, I'm late for an appointment. You do know this is election night? I have an election article to write and a feature to finish by morning or I'm out of a job. I work long hours and get paid half of what I'm worth. But as much as I detest my present situation, I do not intend to risk losing the only job I have to meet with you. Tell me something or this conversation is over."

Travis paused one last time. "Alpine was with Eva the night she disappeared."

Anna emitted a slow groan. "So were two hundred other city employees, until they went home for the evening; everyone did. You evidently didn't do enough homework or you would have known that. Eva had been working alone Christmas Eve. If she left the building with Mr. Alpine, the bogeyman, or anyone else, the surveillance cameras would have seen them. Now if you'll excuse me Mr. Travis--"

"That's because she never left the building."

CHAPTER

2

As a late model Monte Carlo with three men inside pulled up to the curb in front of the French bistro, the driver turned the headlights off. A man got out of the car and ran across the street to check on the Accord parked in the alley. It was Dana Travis's car. Forty minutes later, a white Volvo pulled up to the restaurant. A petite African-Filipino woman got out, entered the restaurant, and took the steps up to the lounge.

Travis was waiting by the bar.

He didn't look anything like what Anna had expected him to. He was five-feet six, obese, with a severe double chin and an uneven gait in his walk caused by bad feet. They sat in a booth in the back. Anna ordered drinks while Travis talked. Fifteen minutes later she had heard enough. She grabbed the bar tab and keys from the table and rose to her feet.

"I have to go, Mr. Travis. I have an early morning deadline."

"I've been telling you the truth."

"That's what you say. You dragged me thirty-five miles down here—tell me some crazy story about Victor Alpine and his campaign manager, Desmond Shaw, and you expect me to believe you without a shred of evidence. I . . ."

"I told you I saw everything. What else do you want?"

"No offense, but you don't impress me as being a very credible witness. You haven't given me a straight answer to any of my questions. You tell me why I don't believe you."

Travis knew she was right. He'd lose her if he couldn't think of something convincing to say.

"Well, I'm waiting."

"Alpine and Shaw take their orders from someone else."

Anna stared at him, "Who?"

"I can't tell you that."

"Bye, Travis."

"If I told you, we would both be dead by morning," he said, squeezing her hand.

"You want me to believe you—give me proof."

He grabbed her hand and led her to the other side of the restaurant. "All the proof you want is in that building across the waterway," he said, pointing out the window at the ominous looking structure suspended in fog.

Anna leaned across the table, straining to see the outline of the silver building marooned at the end of the long pier. "What is that?"

"A cannery, but that's not what it's used for."

There was a good chance he'd been wasting her time, but there was one thing he wasn't lying about. The building looming over the water was definitely not a cannery. Anna sat back down in the booth.

CHAPTER

The first sixteen days of September had been typical "Indian summer" days of sun and warmth—a welcome relief for Washingtonians. Summer had been cooler and wetter than usual and the late reprise of heat had restored the resident's faith in God. He hadn't forgotten His people in the Pacific Northwest after all. It hadn't rained in Evergreen for nineteen consecutive days, but that changed as Anna was halfway home from her meeting with Travis.

Her Volvo came to a halt on the freeway as the rain beat unmercifully against the windshield. Thick sheets of water poured down the windows making it impossible to see. Northbound freeway traffic was at a complete standstill. To the west, Boeing Airfield's blue runway lights were barely visible against the thick rolling fog that was consuming everything in its path.

Traffic appeared to be moving, but it was just an illusion created by the sea of amber taillights flashing against the backdrop of the falling rain. Sounds of smooth jazz played softly on the radio, but Anna wasn't listening. She was too absorbed with her thoughts and paranoia. She didn't see the white Monte Carlo that had pulled alongside her in the other lane.

The rain subsided and traffic began moving again. Anna inched the car forward until she got frustrated and took the next exit off the freeway. Ten minutes later she crossed the lake over to Hunts Point.

She put the car in the garage and hurried inside, shaking the rain water from her hair. Flinging her trench coat over the back of the leather sofa, she headed to the kitchen. Anna turned on the television, latte machine, and checked the answering machine. No calls from Marcus or anyone else for that matter. She worked long hours, had few friends, and no serious man in her life since Marcus.

Anna picked Marcus's photo off the bookshelf. He was the only man she ever loved, but for both of their sakes, she had left him years ago. Now, middle-aged and lonely she seldom dreamed anymore of being married and having children.

Staring out the window, she noticed that the rain was falling heavily again. An anchorman on television was announcing Victor Alpine's successful bid for the Republican nomination for the Senate. She gently rested Marcus's picture back on the shelf and went into the kitchen.

The light on the Braun signaled that her drink was ready. She returned to her desk clutching the hazel nut latte as her thoughts shifted to the disturbing conversation she had with Travis. His story seemed so unbelievable that it bordered on the ridiculous. But as Anna reviewed her notes, the more his story began to make sense—not matter how crazy it sounded. Another sip of the latte didn't do anything to settle her nerves or the sudden fear she felt creeping up her spine. If there was just a shed of truth in what he told her about Victor Alpine and Eva, Anna knew she could be in danger. However, she had little choice.

Eva's unsolved disappearance ten years ago still haunted her. Eva had been her rescuer, mentor, and friend. Even if Travis was lying, Anna owed Eva. She needed to discover the truth and she needed to find Doc.

She lost touch with him since his father's funeral, six years ago in Evergreen, and had no way to contact him. The only person that could was Marcus. She dialed his number in San Francisco, but he didn't answer. She tried his cell phone and got the same response.

Anna was up until midnight finishing her newspaper articles. Wrapping her slender fingers around her third latte, she walked across the room and turned on the gas fireplace. The grinding sound of ball bearings reminded her she still needed to call the repairman. It was only mid-September, but already there was a cool chill in the air. Lying back on the sofa she made another telephone call to Marcus, but he still didn't answer. She went to bed thinking about him, like she did every night before falling asleep. When Marcus returned her call at 5:00 a.m., Anna wasn't alive to answer the phone.

CHAPTER

Travis scratched the stubble on his unshaven face as he paced the floor. Something was wrong. Every few seconds he glanced at the phone on the kitchen wall expecting it to ring, but it didn't. He hadn't heard anything from Anna Mateo, *or* Desmond.

I should've gone into the office today. Staying home will only make him more suspicious. He'll know something's up. His random thoughts were beginning to fray his confidence to the point of wondering if his plan would work. It had been two days since he passed the information to Mateo—more than enough time for her to check out his story. *Something must have gone wrong.* The morning newspaper lay untouched on the kitchen table next to his cup of cold coffee. He quickly thumbed through the pages looking for Anna's column, hoping it might contain some cryptic clue. What he found instead was her obituary.

"Anna Mateo, popular Seattle reporter and columnist for this newspaper was found dead yesterday in her Seattle condominium. The cause of death is unknown, although Seattle detective, Lane Kilgor, has ruled out foul play. All indications are that Ms. Mateo passed away in her sleep."

Travis's hands trembled as he gripped the paper tightly. He poured himself a cup of lukewarm coffee, and mixed it with the last of the whiskey he had stashed over the refrigerator. He emptied the cup and finished the article. His eyes froze on the last paragraph:

"A spokesman for the family, Marcus St. John, said that Ms. Mateo's body will be flown home to Oakland for burial. Memorial services will be held next week at the Seattle Hills Funeral Home."

Travis grabbed the telephone book off the counter and ran his pudgy fingers through the yellow pages until he found the funeral home. He dialed the telephone number and spoke to pleasant women who told him the name of St. John's hotel.

An hour later, he entered the lobby of the Legends Hotel in Seattle carrying a cardboard box. It took him twenty minutes to find a hotel attendant willing to tell him St. John's room number. Travis slipped a twenty-dollar bill into her palm, thanked her, and took the elevator up to the fifth floor. Room 588 was a private suite located at the end of the hallway. Travis wiped his sweaty palms across his pants and tucked in his shirt. For a moment he stood in front of the massive white doors trying to build up the courage to knock on the door. Once he did, it would be too late to turn back. But then he realized that he had no other options now that Anna Mateo was dead. He rapped his knuckles against the door. A tall, attractive redhead answered with a gun in her hand.

"I'd like to speak with Mr. St. John," Travis said.

CHAPTER

The *Seawolf* soared effortlessly as an eagle riding the jet stream. The aqua and banana colored turbocharged seaplane was on its way home from Miami. It leveled out at 9,000 feet as it passed over the harbor and the familiar red-tiled roofs of Charlotte Amalie. The plane banked right, circling the islands before making its approach from the west.

"Boss, it don't get no better than this," Carl said, as he guided the plane down. He and the man he called Doc exchanged smiles, knowing they had the best view of one of the most beautiful cities in the Caribbean. Charlotte Amalie was the capital of the United States Virgin Islands and the busiest cruise-ship harbor in the West Indies. When the seaplane crossed over Botany Bay, Carl switched on the fuel and hydraulic boost pumps, lowered the flaps, and gently touched the plane down on the water. It glided to a smooth stop in front of a waiting launch. "You got yourself a fine plane here, mon. Yessir, this a fine airplane."

"Glad you like it. Feel free to take it up anytime you want."

"You jiven', mon. Really?"

"Really. With school starting tomorrow, I'll be lucky if I can find time to fly her on weekends. She'll just be sitting in the harbor at Christiansted collecting barnacles. You'll be doing me a favor."

The gapped-tooth bow-legged West Indian could barely contain his excitement. "Why you really buy this plane, boss? It just seem a waste of your money."

"We needed it. As often as I travel between the Islands and the mainland, it makes sense to have my own transportation. It's also a good business investment and it'll save us money in the end. We can fly in our own supplies for a fraction of the cost we're paying now. And besides, I know how much you enjoy flying."

Like a kid that had just discovered Disneyland for the first time, Carl's face beamed.

"Now that you will be away from the restaurant more often, maybe you'll finally agree to hire more people to help you before you work yourself to an early grave," Doc said.

"I don't want no help and don't need none. I've been working all my life, mon. A good hard day's work is nourishment for the body and mind. Why you wanna pay someone to do what I can do better?"

"Because you never stop. Take some time and do something fun for a change. When's the last time you had the weekend off?"

"Too much work to do."

"That's what I'm talking about, Carl. Stop being so stubborn and hire a couple of part-time cooks."

"Well, as long as I'm still your manager, I make the business decisions and there won't be no hirin' goin' on." That was the end of the conversation, no more discussion on the subject. Carl was Doc's business manager and father figure. Doc loved him more than he did his own father, which he was ashamed to admit.

Doc shook his head in defeat. He knew no amount of persuasion was going to change Carl's mind, even if it made sense. He draped his arm over the small man's shoulders, and smiled. "Okay, forget it old man. Let's go get some brew."

"Now you finally talkin' some sense, mon."

● ● ●

The harbor boat dropped them off on the pier in front of the restaurant. It was 9:30 in the morning, and already a balmy seventy-six degrees. The waterfront was alive and swarming with tourists spilling onto the dock from the *Caribbean Holiday* and two other luxury cruise ships anchored in the east harbor.

The *Seawolf Cove* was nothing special to look at, but what the former schoolhouse lacked in style and elegance it more than made up for in charm and ambience. The 19th century restaurant was a local favorite where tourists flocked to have generous portions of dolphin, swordfish, and smoked black bean soup, while enjoying the illuminated harbor through the provincial French windows. The hostess greeted the men as they entered and headed straight for the bar.

Doc poured two mugs of *African Spear* from the tap and slid one down the bar to Carl. They raised their mugs in salute to the photograph hanging on the wall over the bar of Gabriel Anderson, Carl's only son, who had died five years before.

Doc found himself paying reverence to his dear friend. "I miss him too, Carl. Gabe would have had a kick seeing you fly again after all these years. Can you imagine the look on his face if he'd seen the stunt you pulled when you buzzed Alexander Hamilton?"

That brought a smile to the old man's face. "He never took to flying very much, did he?" he chuckled.

"No, can't say that he did, but he sure enjoyed seeing you in the air."

"Thanks again, boss."

"For what?"

"For buying the seaplane."

"No problem, glad I could do it." They raised their beer mug again, but this time it was to toast their new acquisition.

Later, they went to the kitchen where Carl sautéed four filets of red snapper in Cruzan rum, and served it over a bed of red beans and rice.

After lunch Doc left for an appointment. He heard Carl barking out orders as he headed down the street.

"Let's pick up the pace around here. The boss don't pay us good money for nothin', mon. Get those lazy bones goin' we got customers to feed."

CHAPTER

Doc walked east along the harbor passing old warehouses that were built by the Danish and French when they had occupied St. Thomas. He crossed the street over to Tolbod Gad and went past Emancipation Park--a solemn reminder of when St. Thomas had been the largest slave market in the world. He passed streets lined with the landmark houses of Charlotte Amalie, with their Dutch doors and Spanish Andalusian-style patios. At Main Street, he ducked through the archway of the old Pissarro Building, where the impressionist painter lived as a child. The trek ended an hour later at the entrance to the University of the Virgin Islands.

A man in his early twenties greeted Doc at the door. "May I help you, sir?"

"Yes, my name is Julian Sebasst. I have an appointment to see the Chancellor."

"Oh yes, Dr. Sebasst, the chancellor is expecting you. Please come in." The eager young student escorted him to the office of Dr. Jordan Chamberlain, Chancellor of the University. He had recently been appointed by the University trustees to fill the vacancy created by the death of the former chancellor. Chamberlain was a tall, slender man in his sixties whose handsome features reminded Doc of a diplomat he once had met in Paris.

"Come in, come in, my friend," Chamberlain said. He shook Doc's hand vigorously, flashing a smile that was intended to disarm, but his eyes were insincere.

"Dr. Sebasst, thank you so much for coming. I have heard so many good things about you. It's a privilege to finally meet you."

"Thank you," Doc replied warily.

"I apologize for asking you to be here on such short notice, especially with classes beginning tomorrow, but I felt it was important to meet you. I like to know my faculty members personally. I feel blessed to have been offered this position and hope that you and I will be able to work together in a cooperative spirit to make this university great. As I already explained to the other professors, I am here in a supportive role to provide you with whatever resources, guidance and mentoring you may need. My vision for this institution is…"

Doc tried hard to pay attention to Chamberlain's monologue, but his whining British accent was grating. The man seemed totally absorbed in his own aggrandizing dribble. Despite his flowery vocabulary he came across as shallow. The university trustees had wisely appointed him acting-chancellor to get him out of their hair.

"And I have assured the trustees that I will turn this university around. If we look at our challenges as opportunities we can overcome all obstacles. I have heard that you are quite the progressive thinker so I welcome your thoughts." Chamberlain leaned back in the chair, fingers laced behind his head, smiling.

Doc had several talents, one of which was the ability to read people. He didn't believe a word Chamberlain said. The man was a native islander and powerful member of the board of trustees. While the trustees had been happy to support him for chancellor, the university faculty and student body had lobbied hard in support of Doc. But in the end, the trustees selected Chamberlain.

"Dr. Chamberlain," he began, "I think we share the same vision for UVI. I too, would like to see this University grow, not only in terms of enrollment, but also in our curriculum and facility development. I'd like to see us improve our library and research resources and post-graduate curriculum."

"Yes, yes. That's all well and good, but I want to know more about you," he said impatiently.

Chamberlain swiveled in his chair and lifted a green folder off the credenza, opening it briskly. "I've been reading your file. Political science degree from Oregon State, Masters and Doctorate in International Relations from George Washington University. Impressive, but certainly not stellar enough to warrant you occupying the second highest position at this university. You had no previous experience in teaching before you came here five years ago. Tell me, Dr. Sebasst, how did you acquire this job?"

Doc was taken back by the sudden rudeness. "I applied for it."

"I will not tolerate flippancy. This is a professional institution and I expect my entire faculty to be civil and honest, or there is no place for them here. Do I make myself clear on this matter?"

So that's what this meeting is about. The man still perceives me as a threat. It was clear to Doc that Chamberlain was baiting him into an argument. Doc didn't answer the question.

Sensing he had gotten the upper hand, Chamberlain played with the knot on his tie as he continued to read Doc's personnel file. "This is preposterous," he said, throwing up his hands. "Aside from your academic record, there is nothing in here about your work history or even where you were born. The only thing we know for sure is that you own a restaurant on St. Thomas," he said in disgust.

"If you're worried about whether I misrepresented myself, the information is easily verifiable. Pick up the phone and call the universities where I earned my degrees."

"Oh, I already did that, and you are who you say you are. The schools remembered you, especially Professor Dalasi at George Washington."

"So what's the problem?"

"*You* are my problem, Dr. Sebasst." He slammed his open hand on the desk. "I want you to answer my questions. Who are you and why doesn't anybody seem to know anything about you? How can a professor on your meager salary afford to spend money like you do on extravagant purchases like that airplane you just bought in Florida?"

Doc fought to control his anger. He leaned forward in his chair. "It's a seaplane. Let's get a few things straight. First of all, what I do with my money and my time outside this institution is none of your business. Second, I'm qualified to teach here and I'm good at what I do. My personal life, including my past, is not up for discussion. I don't have to account to you or anyone else."

"This *is* my business and if you don't give me a straight answer, you will find yourself unemployed," Chamberlain yelled.

Doc stood up and leaned his large frame over the desk. "Jordan," he whispered, "I have a legally binding contract to teach at this university for the next three years, and I expect the university to honor that commitment. I also expect to continue on in my position as Head of Faculty. If for any reason I am removed from my job or undermined by you, I'm going to be very upset. And if I'm upset, you're not going to be happy either, believe me." He closed the personnel file and held it out. "All you need to know about me is in here." He walked out of the office, passing Chamberlain's assistant in the hallway.

"Have a nice evening, Dr. Sebasst."

"Thanks, I intend to." He left through the campus gate and hailed a taxi. "Take me to The French Quarter," he told the driver.

CHAPTER

Asha sat cross-legged, mindlessly flipping through an old Essence Magazine. Her fingers stopped when she saw a picture of a man who reminded her of Doc. The title of the accompanying article read, "When Your Man Leaves You." She thought, *If he does, you'd better get on with your life, sister, because no one but you can take care of you.*

Asha had a lot of experience loving the wrong men. She found most non-communicative, emotionally detached, or more interested in her body and green eyes than her character and brain. They couldn't even complete a declarative sentence without asking her to bed. Eventually she became so self-conscious that she stopped wearing dresses when she discovered men would intentionally let her pass them on the sidewalk so they could gawk at her legs. She had pretty much sworn off men until Doc entered her life five years ago.

She remembered the night he'd first walked into The French Quarter. He wasn't handsome, but not bad looking either, and he was tall. He stood six-five and had a well-tempered body she suspected he maintained for other reasons than vanity. Also there was something else. He observed people and his environment carefully, but in a non-obtrusive way. His wary eyes never stopped working the room as he waited patiently for his table. Asha noticed his exquisite white slacks, shirt, tie, and lapel vest—definitely not island attire. A newspaper and cigar humidor rested on his lap.

When it was his turn to be seated, he asked for a well-lit table, which the hostess found for him in the back. He ordered a patty melt on wheat, fries, and beer. Asha watched him remove reading glasses from his vest pocket and open the newspaper. An hour later he was still absorbed in the paper, very oblivious to the other patrons in the crowded restaurant. Curiosity got the better of her.

She went over to his table, where his face was still buried in the newspaper. "What kind of man comes to the most expensive restaurant in the Islands only to order a burger and French fries?"

He folded the paper and removed his glasses. His suspicious eyes quickly assessed her, and then a slow-forming smile crossed his face. "I don't eat burgers, only distilled versions of them. As for the French Fries—this is a French restaurant isn't it?"

She laughed. "How would you rate the food?"

"Excellent, but overpriced."

"If I had to guess, I'd say money is not one of your major problems."

"It will be if I continue to have to pay twenty-one dollars for a sandwich. Back home I could get the same meal for a quarter of the price."

Asha folded her arms. "And just where is home?"

"Oakland, California."

"Are their patty melt and French fries as good as ours?"

"No."

"I didn't think so. That's why we charge what we do, but I'll take your comments under advisement. My name is Asha Panther, the owner of this burger diner."

Doc stood up and reached for her hand. "Julian Sebasst, but my friends call me Doc. Nice to meet you." The minute he touched her hand Asha was hooked. There was something about the combination of softness and strength that instantly made her feel comfortable and at ease. They sat and talked until the restaurant closed.

Doc had a way of making her feel special without any overt displays of affection or the desire to pursue and conquer. He simply wanted to be her friend, and Asha enjoyed his company. Occasionally, he would stop by when he was in town and they would have quiet dinners together. They talked for hours about everything, except their pasts. Both were sensitive to the pain they saw in each other's eyes when skirting too close to darkly held secrets. Sometimes Asha would cry for no apparent reason and Doc would hold her. The more she saw him, the more she wanted to be with him. One Sunday evening following dinner, she divulged the pain that had tormented her for so many years.

When she was a child living in Santiago, her father had molested her until she ran away from home. At sixteen she borrowed money from an uncle and moved to New Orleans to live with an aunt, who was only interested in exploiting her beauty. Even then, she had already evolved into a statuesque woman, who had inherited her mother's green Venezuelan eyes and her Cuban father's bronzed skin. Her exotic look made her a favorite among local photographers and artists.

It didn't take the aunt long to discover that she could make a lot more money by pimping her niece to the half-dozen men who wanted her. Asha's only alternative was to marry a notorious compulsive gambler, whose favorite pastime was hurting people—especially her. She eventually escaped from him and bought a one-way ticket to the Virgin Islands. For the next couple of years, she tried unsuccessfully to validate her worth by sleeping with any man who showed her genuine affection. All that accomplished was the repression of seventeen years of anger, shame, and remorse that lived in her soul.

That night, Doc comforted her as she cried herself to sleep on the couch. When she woke, his protective arms were still cradling her head like a bear holds a brand new cub. He was still asleep. She studied the contours of his hairless face and head, brushing the back of her hand against the smooth blackness of his skin. When she kissed him lightly, he opened his eyes with a sleepy smile. That was the exact moment she realized that she loved him. She rested her head on his chest and wrapped his arms back around her before going back to sleep.

CHAPTER

Jamal knocked on the door before entering the office. "Miss Panther, Dr. Sebasst just came in. Would you like me to send him up?"

"No, that's okay; tell him I'll be downstairs in a minute." Asha tossed the magazine on the desk and went to freshen up.

Doc saw her coming down the stairs. She looked stunning in her black silk *Liz Claiborne* double-breasted suit and yellow silk crepe shell with a rope weave collar. The eight-button jacket clung to her skin like fine calfskin gloves. Even in Valentino flats she was nearly six-feet tall.

She reached up and circled her arms around his neck, kissing him. "How was the trip?"

"It went well. You okay?"

"Fine, now that you're finally back."

He held her hand while slowly turning her around in a circle.

"What?" she asked with a sheepish smile.

"You look amazing. I really missed you."

"Then why didn't you take me with you to Miami?"

"And have you and Carl slinging spears at each other? I don't think so."

She laughed. "He really doesn't like me, does he?"

"I wouldn't go that far. He's just very competitive and he sees The French Quarter as a threat to our business, and since you're the owner…"

Asha arched her brow. "Let me make sure I understand this. He doesn't dislike me personally or for who I am, but rather for what I have? That's about one of the most ridiculous things I've ever heard."

"Yeah, I know, but he's old school. The restaurant is his life and he wants it to be the best on the island."

"We can't always get what we want." She decided to drop it for the moment. "Are you satisfied with the plane?"

"I haven't flown it yet."

Sometimes Doc surprised and confused her. "You're kidding."

"No. I let Carl do the flight orientation in Kissimmee, while I visited friends in Miami. Once we got in the air, I couldn't pry the stick out of his hand."

Asha laughed as she signaled a waitress to bring them some drinks. Doc told her some more about the trip to Florida, which included visiting Carl's daughter and attending an exhibition football game. What he didn't tell her was that he had also spent four days in Washington with his attorneys before a special panel convened by the Department of Justice.

"When do I get to see the plane?" Asha asked.

"Tonight after dinner, if you like. It's sitting in the harbor right now. I named it after the restaurant. Nothing like free publicity."

The waitress arrived with two Mojito Cuban cocktails and a plate of lobster cakes with Caribbean slaw made of red cabbage, limejuice and sea salt.

"Julian, $350,000 isn't exactly free publicity," she said.

"I know, but it's worth the money," Doc said as he popped one of the small cakes into his mouth.

Asha sipped slowly on her drink, but her eyes didn't leave Doc.

"What's wrong?" he asked.

"Just when I think I'm finally figuring you out, you throw me another curveball."

He stared at her, uncomprehending.

"As long as we've been together, the only thing I've seen you spend money on is me and the clothes on your back. You live in a house occupied by a bed, a relic you call a piano, and your dogs. Then, all at once, you turn around and drop 350K on a man-toy. You don't think that's a little out of character?"

"I don't, but apparently I'm in the minority. Our esteemed university chancellor shares your sentiment. He apparently doesn't care too much for me." He told her about the disastrous meeting with Chamberlain. "Believe me; he'd love to see me leave the university."

Asha gave him a warm smile. "The only thing Jordan Chamberlain cares about is Jordan Chamberlain: his image, and the power his position can bring him. Why else do you think the trustees exiled him from the boardroom to the campus? Chamberlain doesn't care about the students. You however, have a gift for teaching that many others wish they had. The students love you because you have a knack for applying theoretical principals to real world experience. No one has done more for UVI than you. You're a great leader and the faculty and students support you. The trustees were crazy not to appoint you chancellor, but I say forget them. I'll build you your own university."

Doc smiled. "Well, I'm glad *you* have some money, because I'm broke."

"Don't worry, the house will pick up your check tonight," she said, laughing.

For dinner they had a salad of wild mushrooms sautéed in garlic and olive oil, served over mixed baby greens with blue cheese crumbs and roasted walnuts. After their meal they relaxed on the private deck and watched the sun disappear over the horizon.

● ● ●

Afterward, Asha drove Doc to the harbor, where they took the launch out to the seaplane.

In spite of herself, she was impressed. "It's absolutely gorgeous. When are you going to take me for a ride?"

"I've got classes starting tomorrow. How about having breakfast with me next Sunday at the Cove. Afterwards, we'll take a ride around the Islands."

"I'd love it."

"It's a date; I'll call you tomorrow evening." Suddenly he seemed reluctant to leave her. "I really have to go," he said regretfully.

"I know." Her voice was soft, and she moved closer, giving him a long and passionate good-bye kiss. "I love you very much, Dr. Julian Sebasst."

"I love you too."

She stood on the launch and watched the sleek flying boat lift gracefully from the water and head south.

❀ ❀ ❀

Twenty minutes later, *Seawolf* touched down in St. Croix. Doc took his travel bag from the plane and tossed in the Pathfinder, parked in the lot beside the harbor. He took the Melvin H. Evans Highway north, crossed over to Highway 721, and headed through the hilly terrain of the rain forest.

His house was located in the sparsely populated northwest corner of the island. He pulled into the circular driveway in front of his two-bedroom bungalow. Sabu and Taurus met him in the driveway.

"Whoa, easy boys," he said laughing as the large dogs knocked him to the ground and playfully licked his face as he rubbed their heads. "I missed you guys, too." He played with the Great Danes for a few minutes, before picking up two week's worth of newspapers left in a box on the porch.

He tossed the papers on his desk and checked his E-mail. There were several messages, but they would have to wait until morning. Right now all he wanted was a shower and a good night's sleep. It wasn't until he started toward the bedroom that he noticed the light flashing on the answering machine. There was one message, date stamped from two days ago. He pushed the playback button.

"Hi, Doc, this is Caitlin. Marcus has been trying to get in touch with you for days. This is the only number we have for you. Marcus wants you to come home as soon as possible. Anna Mateo has died and Marcus has gone to Seattle to bring her body home."

Doc stood perfectly still for a long moment, trying to keep control over his thoughts. Anna, dead? Why hadn't Caitlin given him the details? There had been something in her voice that made him anxious. In any case, there was only one thing to do.

He called The French Quarter, but Asha had stepped out. "Jamal, tell her that I have to leave town for a while on a family emergency. I'll call her when I get a chance."

"Yes, sir, I'll make sure she gets the message," Jamal said.

After that, he called the airport to schedule a flight out. The next plane to Puerto Rico was in two hours. He'd be in Miami by morning, where he'd catch a non-stop flight to San Francisco. He shaved, showered, and threw some fresh clothes in a duffel bag. He placed his last telephone call to Dr. Chamberlain's office and left a message on the answering machine.

"I have a family emergency at home I have to attend to. Please have one of the other professors cover my class while I'm away."

He put food and water out for Taurus and Sabu, turned off the lights, and jumped in the truck.

CHAPTER

Sammy Spoon was a loser who thought that fate's inexplicable intervention in his life could somehow alter his predetermined destiny. For example, when he found his winning lottery ticket in the dumpster, he figured his luck had changed. He flew to Atlantic City, intending to parley his $25,000 into a windfall, only to lose it on a spin at the roulette wheel. With the little bit of money remaining, he tried to salvage what was left of his vacation. He hopped on a flight to St. Thomas only to wind up sitting alone on a barstool at The French Quarter.

Spoon ordered his fourth drink while bemoaning his current financial situation. He didn't know it, but fate was about to rescue him again. It didn't happen until his sixth drink and by then he could barely see the bar in front of him. What he could see was the exquisite creature who had just entered the lounge. He didn't recognize her at first because her long hair had been replaced with short black curls. But there was no mistaking her identity. He couldn't believe it was her. Spoon ignored the fresh drink on the bar, paid his bill, and damn near broke into a run—all the while thinking he was about to recoup all that he had lost.

When he got back to his hotel room, he placed a call stateside-to Baton Rouge. "I want to talk with Beale."

"So do the IRS, but that don't mean he wanna talk with them. Hold on," said the gruff voice on the end of the line. A few seconds later he returned to the phone. "Beale wants to know what you want."

"Tell him I just seen his wife."

There was a pause. "Boss says you're crazy, how do you know it's her?"

"Ask him how many black women he knows with green eyes and a six-inch scar on the left side of their neck?"

CHAPTER 10

A sleek black and silver Gulfstream with the initials SJS emblazed on the tail wing slowly crossed the tarmac towards the private airport hangar. Marcus St. John watched a Learjet making its approach for takeoff. He reclined against his seat, lit a cigar, and thought about Anna. It had been another exhausting day. First, he had to deal with the red tape of getting her body released into his custody. Then he and Sydney had spent the better part of the afternoon at Anna's house, packing up some of her personal belongings for her family. Later, he met with the county sheriff and the Seattle Metro Department, before cussing them both out. The evening had been capped off by Travis's visit to his hotel room.

Marcus wiped the window with his hand, trying to see past the wet mist and fog that engulfed the airport. If he hadn't known better, he would have sworn he was still in Seattle and not San Francisco. "Just my luck, lousy weather to end a lousy weekend," he said.

Sydney sat in the adjoining seat, working on a crossword puzzle. "So what are you going to do?"

"Doc will be in tonight; I'll talk it over with him and see what he thinks. Meanwhile, let's start collecting information on Shaw and

Alpine, and their two gophers. I want to know everything about them. When they were born, the last time they took a crap…everything."

"Boss, do me a favor: let Seattle Metro handle this one. You've got enemies already; you don't need this additional drama."

"I've done all the talking I'm going to with the police. Once they saw my black ass I knew they wouldn't cooperate. Besides, we don't exactly see eye to eye."

"Okay, so what do we do with the information Travis gave us?"

"I don't know. There's something strange about him. Did you notice how careful he was to show us only what he wanted us to see from that box of his? He knows more then he's saying. Another thing that bothers me—if Anna was killed because of what Travis told her, why isn't he dead, too? I should have pimp-slapped the truth out of him."

He turned his attention back to the window as the airplane rolled into the hangar and came to a stop. Marcus saw Max, his attorney, sitting in the limousine, fumbling with his glasses as he cleaned them. How old was Max now anyway? Sixty-nine, seventy? Marcus couldn't remember. They had been together so long he had forgotten such trivialities. Over the years, Max had proven himself a wise attorney and good friend. He was considered family, as were Sydney and everyone else he cared about, including Anna. He couldn't believe she was gone. Despite what had happened between them, he had always known she was there, somewhere, and he'd found it oddly reassuring. But he hadn't been there when she needed him, and knowing that rekindled many painful memories.

Back in the day, Marcus had loved her as much as any player could love a woman. They'd been childhood friends and high school sweethearts. After graduating, they ended up working together at her uncle's after-hours club, Suntans. Marcus did the bartending and Anna was the bookkeeper. For a while they had a good life together, until Marcus started pimping women out of the back rooms of the club. Nine months later, he quit his job, gave up hustling and moved into the more lucrative business of drug dealing.

They stayed together, but it wasn't long before he stopped coming home. When he did, he was high or just recently released from jail without any other place to go. If Anna had any money left after paying rent, it generally went to feed his habit or pay his bail. The more she tried to help him, the worse he got. A demon raged in him that could only be pacified by excitement and the allure of the streets. She understood his propensity for self-destruction because she had seen it in his siblings. Their father had abandoned the family when Marcus was an infant. Two of his brothers were in prison and his baby sister had died trying to rob a highway diner outside Chico.

Anna eventually left him and moved to Evergreen, Washington to finish school. Marcus ended up on the streets. He was homeless for three years, drifting the back streets and alleys of Oakland and San Francisco, where he hustled, cheated, and stole to survive.

In the summer of 1975, Marcus hit rock bottom. He was living in an old school bus in an auto scrap yard with no money, food, or prospects for getting either. The only thing he still owned was a gun, which he had decided to use on himself. He looked at the reflection of his once handsome face in the broken mirror and saw scabs and sores. Marcus was sick of himself and his life, and he prayed he'd have the courage to pull the trigger.

Providence interrupted as he sat with a gun on his lap. The two men who entered the junkyard didn't see him in the bus. He overheard them talking about a drug deal going down that night on the docks. A 310-pound dealer named Samson was expecting a shipment of heroin on an Algerian tanker. No one in his right mind would even think of messing with him, but Marcus wasn't in his right mind. He couldn't afford to pass up the opportunity. Marcus ambushed the men as they were leaving and ended up taking a bullet for his trouble. He fell off the loading dock into the bay and disappeared.

A few days later he woke up in a hospital near Carmel with a superficial gunshot wound to his head, and no idea how he got there.

He didn't wait around to find out. That evening he escaped and hitched a ride to Los Angeles. A week later he was on the bus to Austin, Texas. The scar above his right eyebrow was a permanent reminder of the past he was determined to forget.

He got a job as a night guard for a small security company in Austin, where he met and later married the owner's daughter, Caitlin Quinn. Marcus spent six years working for his father-in-law, before returning home to San Francisco and starting his own security firm. Ten years later, at the age of forty-four, Marcus St. John was a multi-millionaire and SJS Force was the largest private security company in California.

CHAPTER

Marcus felt Sydney staring at him from behind. He tried to ignore the dull ache in his chest and focus on the present. "What's up, Sydney?"

"What do we do about Devin Leon-Francis?"

Marcus ignored the question.

"Boss?"

"I heard you, Sydney. What about him?"

"If he's involved, we've got major problems."

Marcus turned to face her. "I know. I don't want to tangle with him either--unless I have to."

Sydney's stare turned to a glare.

"Okay, okay, I won't bump heads with him if he don't bump with me! But I'm not the one you need to be warning. If half of what Travis is pitching us is true, Doc will go after Leon-Francis with a vengeance."

"Then your friend will be killed," she said bluntly.

"Yeah, I know that too. And if he is, I'll have to kill Leon-Francis."

Marcus was deadly serious and Sydney knew it. He never made apologies for who or what he was. He could be an astute businessman or a gangster, depending on what the situation called for.

Sydney was the first to exit the plane. Five men in dark suits greeted her by the waiting hearse. She spoke a few words to the driver and walked over to Max's limousine.

Max rolled down the window, sighing. "If I were only forty years younger."

Sydney smiled at the old man and kissed him on the cheek. "Max, forty years ago I wasn't even born and you were still married. When you dump the old broad, let me know."

He laughed. "Good to have you back. How's Marcus holding up?"

"He's doing pretty well, considering. He needs some help on the jet." Max motioned for the men to enter the airplane. "Marcus has got a personal stake in this case, so we're going to have to watch his back."

Max paused, his face etched with concern. "What's up?"

"He thinks Anna was murdered and that some political bigwig in Evergreen with connections and long arms may be involved. If things get too heated, the boss may not be safe. I'll fill you in later."

Max frowned, shifting uneasily. "What aren't you telling me?"

Sydney's mouth twitched as if she'd bitten into a giant sour ball. "We may have to bop with Devin Leon-Francis," she said coolly.

Max placed his glasses back on his face. "Has he lost his mind?"

"You know how he is. He's taking this thing personally."

"Damn!"

With an effort, Sydney kept her voice steady. "Yeah, I don't like it either."

At that moment, the men exited the airplane carrying Anna Mateo's white casket.

CHAPTER

The stretch limousine pulled into a circular driveway and stopped in front of the three-story house in the woods. The chauffer opened the door and Marcus stepped out, wearing a charcoal-gray tailored suit and sunglasses. His hair and mustache showed traces of white, which added a distinguishing flair to his handsome features. He was slim, fit, and looked taller than his six-foot frame.

Caitlin was waiting for him at the door. "Hi, babe. How was the trip?" She pecked him on the cheek.

He removed the silver toothpick from his mouth. "A little tired, but I'm okay. How are the kids?"

"Fine, they're out back. Did everything go okay?"

"I suppose. I sent Anna's body over to Wintergreen Mortuary. Has her family arrived yet?"

"Her father came in this morning from Manila. The sisters and her brother will get in tomorrow before the funeral."

"And Doc?"

"Late tonight."

"Good." He stared past her with a blankness that still revealed the hurt he felt. Caitlin softly touched his face with her hand. He smiled and gave her an affectionate kiss. "I need to talk some business with Max and Sydney."

"Okay, but don't make it too long. The kids are anxious to see you."

●   ●   ●

Marcus slung his coat over a barstool before pouring himself a drink and opening the double doors leading to the backyard terrace. He removed the gun holster from his shoulder and placed the twin automatic pistols in the desk drawer of his African mahogany desk. In the middle of the room were three oversized couches arranged in a U in front of the adobe fireplace. Marcus sat on the couch and propped his feet on one of the ottomans while he waited for Sydney and Max to show up. When they arrived, each occupied a separate couch. Sydney kicked her boots off and curled up to get comfortable. Max sat rigid as a new student attending his first day of class, and just as uneasy.

Marcus reached for the cigar box on the corner table. "What's on your mind, Max?"

"I'm just concerned that you're taking this thing a little too far."

"What do you mean?"

"Sydney told me what you're up to. Tell the police what you know and let them take care of it; you've got enough problems to deal with already."

"I can't just walk away from this."

"Why?"

"You know why. Anna was like family to me. She saved my sorry ass on more than one occasion. The least I owe her is to find out what really happened, and that's what I intend to do."

"Her death was accidental, wasn't it?" Max asked.

"Only if you believe the police reports, which I don't. They say the flue fan in her gas fireplace malfunctioned and that carbon monoxide backed up in the room, knocked her out, and eventually killed her. I checked out the fireplace myself. The fan didn't work because someone cut the damn wires. I call that damn suspicious. Obviously the police didn't, because they weren't interested in anything I had to say."

"Why would they help cover up her murder?"

Marcus had considered the question, and there seemed to be only one answer. "Because they're in on it."

"You can't believe that."

"Yeah, I can, after what Travis told us. The only people I trust are in this room. Everyone else is suspect, especially the Evergreen Police." Marcus removed a notepad from his suit pocket and handed it to Max.

"What's this?"

"Anna's notes from a meeting she had with a guy named Travis. I found it wedged between the cushions of her couch. If the police were really serious about the investigation, they would have bothered to search her place."

Max turned the notepad over in his hand, afraid to open it. "What's in it? No, don't tell me, I don't want to know." He tossed it back. "As your attorney and friend I'm telling you, Marcus, you're treading on thin ice. You're telling me you trespassed on a crime scene and stole a potential key piece of evidence? At the very least you could be charged with withholding evidence in an investigation or obstruction of justice."

"What investigation? The police have already closed the case."

Max gave him one of those paternal looks that fathers give sons when they've said something particularly stupid. "You know what I mean. We're not a detective agency and we don't have the resources for this."

Marcus smiled. "I've dealt with bigger problems. Remember the Davenport case? LAPD never would have moved on him if I hadn't broken the case for them."

"Yes, and you almost got your butt shot off in the process," Sydney reminded him.

"That's why I pay you the big bucks to watch my back."

"The bucks aren't that big, boss," she said.

Max was getting irritated; fear did that to him. "This isn't funny. You're dealing with something a whole lot more dangerous than a small-time hood trying to shave points off a basketball game. You could be going up against a would-be U.S. Senator, not to mention the Prince of Darkness himself."

Marcus glanced at Sydney. He'd known this was coming. "I see you told him about Leon-Francis."

"Well, you said I should fill him in on what happened."

Marcus took a long drag on the cigar before speaking. "Look, Max, at this point we don't know if Leon-Francis is involved in this thing or not. All we have is the word of a man I don't trust fully."

"What if he is involved?" Max asked.

Marcus rested the cigar on the ashtray. "You and I have been through a lot together. You've been more of a father to me than my own and I love you. I don't expect you to understand how strongly I feel about what I'm doing. Hell, if our places were reversed, I'd be saying the same things to you. But if this goes all the way up to Leon-Francis's front gate, then so be it. He'll pay too." He picked up the cigar and began smoking again.

Max looked at Sydney in pleading desperation. She shrugged her shoulders, conveying the hopelessness of the situation. Once the boss made up his mind to do something, nothing short of the Second Coming was going to stop him.

Max massaged his forehead with his fingers. "Marcus, I have always admired and even envied the loyalty you show your friends, and like I said, I understand why you may want to exact some measure of justice against the people responsible for Anna's death. But you can't go around stirring up trouble with Leon-Francis. Our security could protect you day and night, and you'd still be no match for someone like him. He's got eyes and ears everywhere. He knows when you need to piss before you do, for heaven sakes."

"I don't intend to jeopardize the welfare and safety of my people over a personal matter. Doc and I will handle this."

"You're not going anywhere without me. I would take personal offense if you met your Maker on my watch," Sydney insisted.

Max looked from one to the other. "I think you're both crazy." He loosened his tie and breathed a heavy sigh of frustration. "I hope your friend Sebasst can talk some sense into you."

"Don't bet on it."

"Since you won't listen to me and are determined to do this thing, I might as well tag along with you. Heaven knows you're going to need all the help you can get to keep your butt out of a sling. What can I do?"

Marcus handed him Anna's notepad. "First, I want you to read her notes. They pretty much confirm what Travis told me. Then I want you to check him out, and a guy named Desmond Shaw—Victor Alpine's campaign manager."

"Okay, I'll get some people on it. What's Shaw got to do with any of this?"

"Travis says he's got a lot of clout and he's not shy about showing his muscle. He owns a large development company in Evergreen--a subsidiary of the Excalibur Group, a land development corporation, owned by Leon-Francis. Supposedly, Leon-Francis is using Shaw to funnel illegal funds into Alpine's campaign coffers."

Max laughed. "What possible interest could Leon-Francis have in Victor Alpine? Even if he's elected to the Senate, he won't last long. Alpine is as old as dirt, which puts him about ten years older than me."

Marcus had been thinking the same thing. "I don't know and Travis won't say, but I'm sure there's a big payout if Leon-Francis is mucking around in it."

"That's ridiculous. He has more money and power than most Third World dictators." Max said.

"I told you Travis fed me some strange stuff," Marcus said.

"Even if it's true, that seems like a pretty flimsy excuse to kill someone," Sydney said.

"Not if they thought Anna might expose the truth," Marcus said.

"Why didn't Travis go to the police?" Max asked.

"The same reason I wouldn't, if I thought they were involved," Marcus said.

"Oh, but he doesn't have a problem spilling his guts to Anna Mateo or you, a man he's never met before in his life. I don't buy it; the man is pulling your chain, Marcus," Max said.

"Maybe, but if you'd seen the expression on his face when he talked to us last night, you might not think so. The guy was scared to death. He could hardly mention Leon-Francis's name without pissing all over himself. The little information he gave me is nothing compared to what he knows. We just have to figure out what he's not telling us."

Sydney sat up and started putting on her boots. "How do we do that?"

"I think I'll let Doc take a crack at him. He might have better luck. Meanwhile, we'll go with the information we have and start digging for more."

"Anna Mateo's message mentioned that Travis knew something about Eva Ward's disappearance. What did he tell you?" Max asked.

"Only that the Evergreen Police were also involved in that cover-up. He gave me the name of the chief investigative officer."

"That was over ten years ago. Is he still around?"

"Yeah, his name is Lane Kilgor, but he's no longer with the Evergreen Police. He's a detective for Seattle Metro, and he's also the investigating officer in Anna's death."

CHAPTER

"You've been up for hours. Lie down," Caitlin said as she gently pushed her husband back on the bed.

Marcus's meeting with Max and Sydney had lasted over an hour and then he spent another two hours playing with his daughters. Afterwards, they coaxed him into reading two bedtime stories before he was released to the sanctity of his bedroom.

Caitlin gently massaged his temples with her fingertips. "It'll be good to see Doc again."

"Yeah, I can't believe I haven't seen him for years."

"He looks the same," she reassured him.

"How would you know?"

"Remember, I saw him last year when he had a layover, while you were in New York. Doc hadn't changed a bit—he still looks good."

Marcus pulled her close. "Yeah, but does he look as good as me?"

"Baby, you get better looking the longer I'm with you."

He laughed, then reached up and kissed her tenderly on the lips. "You definitely have one advantage; you don't suppress your feelings, and as far as I know, you've never kept secrets from me. Doc, on the other hand, will talk about everything under the sun except himself. He only lets you get so close to him."

"Doc's a quiet dude. That doesn't mean he has no emotions. I certainly have no problem communicating with him," he said, rolling over on his stomach.

"That's because you two don't talk about anything substantive except the good old days—never about what's really going on in your lives."

"Doc likes his privacy."

"I would think being a university professor would be exciting and rewarding, but he never talks about it unless you ask. You have to pry every ounce of information from him. That's not natural for a man."

"It is for him. Maybe he just doesn't like inquisitive white girls asking him about his shit."

She slapped him on the head. "Oww! What exactly is it you want to know?"

"For starters, I'd still like to know where he got the money--"

"Caitlin, don't start that again."

"I know you're curious, too."

"Maybe, but unlike you, I don't care. If he hadn't bailed us out when he did, we wouldn't be having this discussion, there would be no SJS, and that space on the wall holding your law degree would still be empty."

"Don't get me wrong, honey. I, more than anyone, appreciate what he's done for us, but I just can't help thinking he may have done something illegal." Caitlin propped herself on her elbow. "A half million dollars is no small amount."

"Doc lives like a pauper, at least compared to everyone else in the civilized world. He probably still has the first dollar he ever made, and I'm sure he does well at teaching."

"He's only been at the university for five or six years. What was he doing before that?"

"He lived in Europe for about fifteen years."

"Doing what?" she persisted.

"Don't know and, frankly, don't care," Marcus said with a note of irritation in his voice. "Caitlin, you're starting to sound like a prosecutor. I'm not saying Doc is perfect or that he doesn't have any larceny in him. We both traveled the same path, but the difference between us is that his father kept his ass in line, and Doc didn't make the same stupid mistakes I did. He's no saint by a long ways, and the boy can go buck wild when pressed, but believe me—he's as straight as his old man."

"Well, I still think he's got some issues to work out."

"Now *that* we can agree on. He's got God problems and those are a lot worse than issues."

"What?"

"God problems. You know the kind that only the Almighty can help you with and that's assuming he's even on your side. Doc had a special calling like his dad to be a preacher, but he didn't want to hear any of that noise. He had his life already mapped out, and he wasn't planning on changing it for anyone, including God. Even a Philistine like me has enough sense not to mess with the Man, but not Doc—always been stubborn. Has to do everything his way."

She just couldn't let it drop. "What kind of work did he do before he moved to Europe?"

"Don't know. I never asked. If Doc wanted me to know, he would have told me. Otherwise, I stay out of his business and so should you."

"How can you be like that, Marcus? He's your friend; don't you care?"

"Look," he lifted his head off the pillow to look at her. "What's the deal anyway? Why do you care so much?"

"Because he's your best friend and I love him too. I want him to be happy and I know he isn't, but you wouldn't understand; you're a man."

Marcus flopped back on the bed. "*Whatever.*"

CHAPTER

Doc had to wait forty minutes for the baggage carousal to spit his duffle bag out. It took him another twenty minutes to make it from Terminal Two down to West Field Road and the rental car center. When he got there, all he found were long lines of disgruntled travelers being turned away because there were no more cars. He went outside and felt like he had just stepped into an airport under siege. There were hundreds of stranded and angry passengers on the verge of rioting because the shuttles weren't coming fast enough and there were too few cabs. The police were out in force, but were under manned.

What in the world is going on? He wondered, just as he was about to go back into the airport, he felt a touch on his shoulder.

"Excuse me, are you Julian Sebasst?"

Doc turned around to see a woman holding a sign with his name on it. "My name is Sydney Belleshota. I've got a car waiting for us on the next level."

Doc shook her hand. "Pleased to meet you, Sydney. I've never seen the airport this busy before. What's going on?"

"The National Rifle Association's in town for their annual conference. Most of the yahoos here are probably attending."

They took the escalator up to the parking garage, where people were being herded through a makeshift security checkpoint. A courteous policeman ushered them past.

"What's up with all the security?" Doc asked.

"I suppose they're worried that some of the yahoos might take a crack at our illustrative vice president."

Doc had forgotten that Vice President Lauren Dillon was in San Francisco for the weekend. "It's ironic that the NRA is in town the same time their most ardent foe is here too," he said.

"Yeah, the good old boys would love to chat with her over her gun control legislation."

"Sounds to me like you're less than enamored with the woman yourself."

"She can't help it if she's an idiot, and that she's incoherent most of the time and inconsistent all the time. Her abysmal performance at the Mideast Summit was an embarrassment to the country and a disgrace to Jews. Why the President ever picked her as his VP is beyond me."

"Because women loved her."

"Feminists maybe, but what does that tell you? They're about as in touch with mainstream America as Rush Limbaugh. If I had my way, I'd give them all guns and let them go at it with the yahoos. Winner takes all—if there are any spoils left. With any luck, they'd all bump each other off."

Doc laughed. "Crude, but an effective way to deal with dissidents. By the way, how did you recognize me?"

"Mr. St. John pays me to know these things."

A limousine pulled up beside them. They got in and Sydney immediately slipped out of her suit coat and relaxed. A Berretta dangled from a holster underneath her arm. She reached for a bottle of Tanqueray off the bar. "Want one?"

"No, thanks. Is it just my imagination or does everyone carry a gun in this city?"

"I can't speak for my fellow San Franciscans, but mine comes with the job—and I'm paranoid."

"Mind if I have a look at it?"

Sydney pulled the Berretta from its holster and handed it to him. He admired the intricate oak leaf design on the silver-plated barrel and handgrip. He had seen a pair of guns like this once before—on display at the War Museum. The *Mossad,* Israel's secret service, had donated them to the museum. He flipped the gun over and handed it back to her. "Nice. Where did you get it?"

"A gun shop in Los Angeles."

"And what exactly do you do for Quik?"

"Quik?"

"Marcus. It's his childhood nickname."

"Security," she said.

"Aren't you a little undersized for that kind of work?"

She laughed. "Isn't your real question, "What is a thirty-one year-old girl, who drinks double shots of gin, doing working in security?"

Doc stared at the young redhead with the short-shingled haircut. She had a girlish smile on an oval face with long, widening dark brows. But the most noticeable thing about her was the intensity of her cobalt eyes; they were haunting and filled with introspection. Sydney was older and wiser than she appeared and, Doc thought, probably good at judging character. "Sorry, I didn't mean to offend you."

"No offense taken," she said, pouring another drink before settling back against the seat. She noticed the humidor Doc had resting on the seat beside him. "You mind if I try one of your cigars?"

"Sure." He passed her a *Silvateo* and lit it.

"Thank you." She rolled the Havana cigar in her mouth, puffing lightly a few times before taking two long drags. A smile creased her face. "How did you manage to get your hands on these, Dr. Sebasst?"

"I have a friend in high places, and please call me Julian or Doc."

"Do those friends just happen to work in customs?"

"My secret."

Her always-assessing eyes narrowed. "You know I could turn you in for being in possession of illegal contraband?"

"Yes, but then you would have to explain where you really got that little gun of yours."

Sydney held his stare for a moment before she smiled broadly. She took another puff of the cigar.

The limousine turned left off the main road onto a private street lined with large maples whose arched limbs formed a tunnel over the roadway leading up to the front gate.

At the opposite end of the St. John estate, near the back gate, a rented van was hidden under the cover of old growth trees. Inside sat six men who had arrived in California earlier that day on a private plane from Evergreen. Now they were waiting for their orders.

CHAPTER

Marcus was waiting when his old friend stepped out of the limo. He greeted Doc with a wide smile and a hug. "Hey, bro, nice to see you home."

"You too, Quik."

Sydney closed the car door and started across the lawn toward the guesthouse.

"Thanks, Sydney," Marcus said.

"I'll see you tomorrow, boss. Nice to have met you, Julian. Don't forget the cigars."

"What's up with that?" Marcus asked.

"I promised her a box of my favorites."

Marcus chuckled. "The girl does have some strange habits."

"She's definitely one of the most unusual women I've ever met."

"She's one of the best people I have. That's why she's our security chief."

Doc stared at him in surprise. "You're joking."

"Don't let her size and age fool you. She's gotten me out of a jam more than once."

●   ●   ●

They went upstairs to the study where Marcus mixed them some drinks. He passed one over to Doc.

"Thanks, but I quit drinking."

"Good—more for me." He placed the drinks on the desk and took a seat. He slid the cigar box across the desk.

"No thanks, I'm fine." Doc rested against the recliner and closed his eyes.

Marcus started laughing. "You need *something*. You look like the walking dead. When's the last time you slept?"

"We'll have all the time in the world to rest once we're dead."

"Man, you sound just like your old man. Remember that kryptonite sermon he gave us that day on your front porch? I'm telling you that would have dropped Superman to his knees."

Doc's eyes gleamed. "You mean the one where he said, 'You boys don't know how blessed you are by Jesus. He has given you both an abundance of intelligence, talent, and skill. Using those wonderful gifts to glorify His name is the very least you owe him.'"

Marcus slammed his palm down on the desk. "You sound just like him, too! I'm telling you, Doc, you got the calling."

"Don't start with me, Quik; I'm not in the mood."

"Man, when are you going to wake up and stop fighting it? You're not ever gonna win. Who was that cat in the bible that fought with God?"

"Jacob."

"Yeah, Jacob. He stayed up all night wrestling with Him, and he was a *bad* brother, but did he win? No."

"I've been at it longer. I figure my odds are getting better."

"Boy, for someone as smart as you, how can you be so dumb? You're gonna mess around and the Lord is gonna put a Jonah on your butt. You'll wake up one day and find yourself in the belly of the whale with all those other hardheaded, disobedient heretics."

"And I suppose you're doing the Lord's work."

"I don't have the patience to deal with these worldly fools. The

Lord has to have some disciples like me to help people repent the error of their ways."

They joked and laughed for a while before the conversation turned serious.

"I'm glad you came. It probably wasn't easy to drop everything."

Doc shook his head. "I know how much Anna meant to you. I had to be here."

"Yeah, I appreciate it." Marcus stared intently into his drink, swirling it slowly. Finally he cleared his throat. "There's something Caitlin didn't tell you. Another reason you need to be here. Anna left a message for me Sunday night saying she had information on your sister's disappearance."

Doc pulled the recliner upright and leaned forward, his eyes fixed on Marcus. He hadn't thought about Eva in a long time, and suddenly the grief was new again. But he pushed it aside—along with the guilt.

Marcus swallowed his rum and explained about Travis, Alpine and Shaw.

"Travis says Shaw had Anna killed because she found out about illegal money being laundered through Alpine's campaign. According to Travis, Shaw has carved out a mini-empire in Evergreen. He has power over everything, including Victor Alpine, and nothing happens in the city he doesn't know about. Travis swears he has names, dates, and copies of illegal transactions involving the exchange of money between Shaw and Alpine."

"Why doesn't he go to the police?"

"He doesn't trust the police; says Shaw controls them. Anyway, it would be tough to prove anything. Shaw washes the money through an assortment of businesses before it finds its way into Alpine's treasury. Travis says his set-up is so tight it would take accountants years to work through the labyrinth of false records and accounts."

"Do you believe him?"

"There's probably some truth in it, but it's hard to tell."

Doc sat rigid and asked the question he was not sure he wanted answered. "What happened to Eva?"

"He wouldn't talk about her at all. I think maybe he used her to lure Anna in."

Leaning back, deflated, Doc reached for the cigar he didn't have.

"Sorry." Marcus wanted to comfort his friend, but didn't know how. He decided to continue. "I can't even get a straight answer out of him about Anna or why he's telling me all this shit. When I press him for some answers, he gets nervous and wants to leave. He tells me Shaw's men are tailing him. The next thing I know, he takes my business card and says he'll stay in touch. Before I can blink, he splits out the door. I thought you might want to talk to him."

"You got that right." His tone was steady, but the tense muscles around his nose and mouth revealed his disquiet. "What else do you have?"

Marcus gave him Anna's notepad. "Her notes say that a detective named Kilgor and some retired Army Colonel do Shaw's dirty work. I don't know the Colonel, but I met Kilgor. He's about as bad as they come, and he just happened to be the investigating detective on Eva's and Anna's cases."

Doc flipped through Anna's notebook. "Anna says here that Travis has worked for Shaw for twenty-two years."

"Travis was his senior accountant. He says he quit because Shaw became suspicious and didn't trust him anymore."

Doc narrowed his eyes. "Something smells and it's not fish. Why, after all these years, has he decided to expose Shaw?"

"Told you—he's not telling us the real deal." Marcus flicked the ash from his cigar. "So what do you think?"

"He could be blackmailing Shaw or Alpine, or both." As difficult as it was to concentrate, Doc forced himself to think. "That could explain why he's still walking around breathing. Of course that's assuming anything he said is true. He could have played Anna and is trying to do the same to you. I don't know what he wants, but it sounds like he needs you to help get whatever he's after. He's leading this dance and I guess you're going to have to follow, if you want to know the reason."

Marcus guzzled down his drink and got up for another. Doc reached across the desk and grabbed a pencil. His thoughts drifted to Asha. He hadn't talked to her since he left St. Croix. He wondered why he'd never told her about Eva or his father. Perhaps because he was acutely aware of how badly he had failed both. He missed Asha suddenly, and inadvertently mumbled her name.

"What did you say?" Marcus asked as he sat back down.

"Nothing. I was just thinking about my lady."

"The same one you've been seeing for a while?"

Doc nodded.

"Oh." Marcus didn't know how else to respond. All he could hear was Caitlin's prophetic words: *See, you men can't deal with emotions.* "So, you have any other theories?"

"It takes a lot of money to run a Senate campaign. If Alpine is receiving illegal contributions, where are they coming from?"

"Travis says it's a man named Leon-Francis. Devin Leon-Francis."

"Never heard of him."

"I'm not surprised. He's not a person you want for an enemy. His people worked the Oscars last year."

"He's in the security business too?" Doc asked.

"Among other things. If something makes money, he owns or controls a piece of the action. Telecommunications, oil, aerospace research, real estate, computers, and movies. The list is endless. One of his companies is a land development company known as the Excalibur Group, which is located in San Diego where he supposedly lives. Travis says Excalibur is bankrolling Alpine's election."

Doc stared at the floor deep in thought. "Money is one thing. Hiding and shuffling it around without anyone noticing is another. Does Leon-Francis have that kind of juice?"

Marcus shifted uncomfortably in his chair. "Yeah, he's one of the most powerful men in America, but don't bother searching for him on Forbes list. Most people haven't heard of him; he's become an expert at staying invisible. He's got a heavy rep and it's not just in business."

Looking up in surprise, Doc asked, "This guy scares you?"

Marcus took a quick sip of rum and rose again. He unlocked one of the file cabinets and retrieved a leather bound dossier, which he dropped on Doc's lap.

"What's this?"

"Everything I know about Leon-Francis. Background stuff, family history—shit like that. You said you never heard of him. How about Basham Stillwater?"

"The 1930's movie mogul who committed suicide?"

"The same. He was Leon-Francis's stepfather. Raised the boy as his own son. It seems two men had seduced Devin's mother, Leona Francis, years before. She got pregnant, had Devin out of wedlock, and both men abandoned her. Stillwater was a competitor of theirs, and they ruined him as well. That's why he blew his brains out. After his death, Leona Francis was committed to a private sanitarium. The fate of Devin Leon-Francis's parents made him the mean, ruthless bastard he is today."

Doc listened intently, taking it all in, wondering why Marcus was telling him all this.

"When he reached 21, Leon-Francis inherited his daddy's two million dollar trust fund and began building his empire. In 1961, his mother died in the sanitarium, having never recovered from her husband's death. Around that time, Leon-Francis dropped out of sight. No one saw or heard from him for years. It was like he had become invisible.

"Eventually, the two men who had forced Stillwater into bankruptcy found their successful movie studios involved in hostile takeovers by foreign corporations. Both studios were liquidated and dismantled, and the men were never heard from again.

Marcus rose from his chair and sat on the corner of the desk, nursing the drink in his hand. "There was never any proof, but lots of people believe Leon-Francis was behind it."

Doc thumbed through the 312-page dossier. "Does he have any other family?"

"A wife and daughter, supposedly. He's fiercely protective of both, and I emphasize the word fiercely. It's rumored that he once buried two guys alive in the Nevada desert after they tried to kidnap his daughter. I've been in this business a long time, and I've heard a lot of stories, but none compare to the ones about Devin Leon-Francis—and none of them are good."

Rubbing his chin pensively, Doc said, "Go on."

"One tale involves the Sampas."

"The crime family that used to operate out of New Orleans?"

"Yeah. Seems like Big Daddy Tippi Sampa and Leon-Francis crossed paths years ago. Leon-Francis was beginning to exert his influence in less than legitimate enterprises, in territory controlled by the Sampas. They tried to kill him and failed. Leon-Francis went to war. Tippi Sampa's four sons were the first to go, then the uncles and cousins, and then Tippi.

"Apparently Leon-Francis wiped out the entire male line. Of course all the deaths were officially listed as accidents—suicides, auto accidents, overdoses, falls from observation towers and amusement rides, shit like that. In all, twenty-two were permanently retired."

Doc was feeling distinctly uneasy.

Taking a deep breath, Marcus continued. "You asked me if the man scares me. Let's just say he's the last person I want to knock heads with. He's always two steps ahead of everyone else, and he always strikes when you least expect it. By the time you figure out what's happening, your head's spinning in your ass, and you're wondering how it got there."

"How come the feds haven't caught up with him yet?"

"Like I said, he's invisible—he flies under the radar. He gets other people to do his dirty work."

"If he's such a phantom, how do you know so much about him?"

"In my line of business I need to know my enemies, and *potential* enemies."

Doc closed the dossier and handed it back to him. "You sure know how to pick your fights. If half of what Travis told you is true, and if Leon-Francis is behind this, he won't be sitting around waiting to see what you do. He'll come after you."

"Look, I don't care whether they want to resurrect the Third Reich or rule the world. That's their business. All I wanna do is get the person who killed Anna."

Doc sighed. In some ways, Marcus was always predictable. He refused to give up a fight, no matter the risks—especially if it involved someone he cared about. But that also meant he could be reckless. "And I want to know what happened to Eva. But in order to find out, we have to care who our enemies are. We have to have a plan. It seems to me that we should start with Travis. Maybe you should find out more about Leon-Francis."

Marcus reached over, opened his desk drawer, and handed Doc a gun. "Here, take it. Why don't you just shoot my black ass now and save Leon-Francis the trouble."

Doc's expression was grim. "As I see it, you don't have a choice. Leon-Francis's people probably already know you met with Travis. The only reason he's probably still be alive is because of what he has on Shaw and Alpine. If that's the case, you need to know what he knows, so you can stay alive too. You say Leon-Francis is invisible. Well, even the Invisible Man had his weak spot, and they got *him*."

"Yeah, but not before he whacked a bunch of suckers first."

＊　＊　＊

The man in the passenger seat of the van adjusted his headset. "I can't hear what they're saying. Play it back."

A second man re-wound the tape and started it again.

"That's better."

Another man was lying on the roof of the van with a telescopic scope, watching Marcus open the double French doors to the terrace. "I got him," he whispered into his headset. "Number one is a sitting duck." He lined-up the cross hairs on the center of Marcus's forehead. "Do you want me to take him out now?"

"Not yet, hold," said the man in the van. He switched radio frequencies and contacted the other shooter in the woods. "Sarge, do you have number two in sight yet?"

"Affirmative, he's still sitting in the chair. Is it a go?"

"Continue to hold. I'm waiting for confirmation."

The satellite phone rang and he picked it up. The message was short. "Negative, it's a no go. Pack it in."

The shooter collapsed the rifle stand and jumped to the ground. "What's wrong? I had him dead-to-center."

"We can't hit them now."

"Why?"

"Orders from Evergreen. St. John's friend is untouchable. Where's Sarge?"

Sarge sprinted out of the woods and jumped into the open cargo door. No one saw the rifle cartridge fall from his flax jacket.

CHAPTER

16

The Lexus crossed the Narrows Bridge to the seaside town of Bayview Harbor. The car turned into Narrow Heights Estates and stopped in front of one of the new executive houses on Harbormaster Ridge, owned by Shaw Development Company.

Desmond Shaw looked around to make sure he was alone before using the passkey to enter the house. He walked through the foyer and up the redwood staircase to the family room, where the spiraled steps took him to the third level. The top floor was a private office built for security for executives working from home. The walls and door were reinforced with two-inch thick concrete. Shaw stuck his security card in the wall and opened the door that entered into the executive suite.

Victor Alpine and the Colonel sat at the round mahogany conference table in the middle of the room, while Lance Kilgor sat behind the L-shaped desk in the corner with his feet propped up on the credenza, smoking.

Desmond cut an imposing figure standing in the doorway. He was six-seven, wore a gabardine duster, Italian calfskin shoes, and sunglasses. His mousse dark hair draped over his ears and rested on his shoulders. He was an improved version of Madison Avenue's Marlboro Man with an extreme attitude. Shaw removed his Chaps duster, folded it, and carefully laid it over the back of one of the leather captain chairs.

Alpine expected him to say something, but he didn't. He couldn't stand the suspense any longer. "Damn it, Desmond, what happened?"

A broad smile flashed across Shaw's face as he took a seat at the table. "Lauren Dillon is finished."

"Yes!" Kilgor shouted, slamming his flabby palm down on the desk. He jumped up and came over to the table toting his ashtray with him.

The Colonel reached over and gave Alpine a congratulatory slap on the back that nearly knocked the elderly man from his chair.

"Are you sure?" Alpine asked as he steadied himself back in the chair.

Shaw crossed his legs. "The President himself confirmed it. You're at the top of a short list of his choices for Vice President. This time next year, you'll be in Washington, and Dillon will be back in Boston where she belongs." Shaw was pleased with himself, and it showed.

Victor Alpine broke out in a smile. "What did they say?" He gushed.

"He's looking for someone who can restore integrity to the office and solidify the party. He wants a moderate who can articulate his vision and help him win the election in two years. You're that man if you can win the Senate seat in two months. Do that and you'll be the next Vice President of the United States," Shaw said, patting Alpine's hand.

Alpine released a loud sigh of relief and then flashed a two-thumbs up salute. "Thanks, Desmond." He relaxed his head back on the headrest. It had taken him years to get to this point, but now he had made it.

Shaw knew what he was thinking. "We're not home free yet, and there's work to be done. We still have to win a senate race and deal with Travis."

Kilgor scratched the itch in his ear with his finger. "I told you we should've handled that little creep a long time ago," he snorted, while flicking the particle of ear wax off his finger. "He's running his mouth too damn much. First that Times reporter and now to that black jungle bunny in California. He's got to be stopped."

The Colonel rose slowly tugging the hem of his neatly pressed military jacket. Even though he was no longer in the army, he continued to prefer his military uniform over civilian clothes. I'm afraid Kilgor is right. Containment is getting more difficult. I don't know who these guys are, but they're starting to piece this together, fast. The sooner we put a cork in it, the better I'll sleep."

"Give Travis what he wants and be done with it. We can afford the money," Alpine said, confidently.

Shaw shook his head. "I don't trust him anymore, and neither should you. If we give in now, he'll only come back to bite us again. And next time you'll be in office and there's no telling what he'll demand. Kilgor and the Colonel are right; we have no choice now but to eliminate him before he has a chance to talk to anybody else."

Alpine wrung his hands. "There has to be another way."

"Believe me, if I thought there was another way out of this mess I would take it. But there isn't, unless you'd rather live in prison instead of the White House. This is not the time to get squeamish, Victor."

"I know, but first the reporter and now Travis? Isn't this a bit risky? Maybe you should try to reason with him again. I just think it would be better--"

Shaw was annoyed, and didn't bother to hide it. "Stop rambling, I know what you think. You think if you ignore the problem it'll go away. Well, it won't. This man can't be reasoned with. He'll destroy us all if we don't stop him."

"Not if we give him the--"

"Damn Victor, have you listened to anything I've said? The man is a manipulative snake. Don't you see that? He'd double-cross God if it would benefit him. He's got us by the throat and he's ready to choke us to death, and you want to kiss and make up with him? He can put you away forever with all the garbage he has on us. Remember that. Don't start believing your own press about how great you are."

Alpine flushed.

"What about the financial books? We still don't know where he's hiding them. We've checked everywhere: his house, the office, even his mini-storage locker on the tide flats. We keep coming up empty," Kilgore interjected.

Shaw pulled his planner out of his coat and tore off a sheet of paper. "Travis is a creature of habit. Every other Wednesday he goes to his bank." He passed Kilgor the paper. "He'll be there tomorrow, so follow him. He may have a safe deposit box."

Kilgor frowned, but stuffed the paper in his pocket. "Even if we luck out and find the books, how do we know he doesn't have other copies floating around out there somewhere?"

"I don't, but it won't matter after he's dead. The books will be a moot point after that."

Kilgor pulled a pack of crumpled cigarettes from his jacket with sweaty fingers. "So, how do you want him taken out?" he mumbled as he stuck the cigarette in his mouth.

"I'll leave the details to you. Just make sure he disappears for good. I don't want to be watching television a year from now and find that his body popped up somewhere."

"Does he have any family we need to be concerned about?" Kilgor asked.

"None that'll miss him. "

"What do we do about St. John and Sebasst?"

"Nothing. No one can prove anything once we silence Travis."

The Colonel had been pacing, but he stopped and turned. "I don't like it. These guys are trouble. You should have let my boys finish the job in California when we had the chance."

"Sebasst has friends in Washington. We can't afford any mistakes," Shaw said.

"He's flying here on Thursday to talk to Travis," the Colonel reminded him.

"Is St. John coming too?" Shaw asked.

"No. He said something about going to San Diego to check on some guy named Leon-Francis."

Shaw froze. "Devin Leon-Francis?"

"Yes, that's the name," the Colonel said.

Alpine jumped to his feet, but Shaw restrained him. "I think," he said very slowly, "that I should hear that tape for myself."

The Colonel played the garbled recording for them. When it was finished, Shaw and Victor looked at each other but said nothing.

Kilgor saw the anxiety on their faces. "Who is this Leon-Francis character?"

"A business associate." Shaw kept his cool with an effort. "That's all." He took a shallow breath.

Kilgor waited for him to continue, but Shaw just stared at him appraisingly.

"So what do you want us to do about St. John and Sebasst?"

Shaw thought for a few seconds, taking the new information into account. "Okay, pop them, but I want it done quickly and right, *before* they have a chance to talk to anyone. It has to look like an accident. I don't want any possibility of the feds connecting us to this. Sebasst is U.S. Treasury, and they'll be all over our asses if you screw it up."

The Colonel coughed and fanned Kilgor's cigarette smoke away in disgust. He disliked the undisciplined, overweight detective, especially when he was in chain smoking mode. He moved away from the table again. "Sebasst is a treasury agent?"

"Former Secret Service. He got into some trouble awhile back and left the service, but he's still connected. He left D.C. after that and now lives in the Caribbean."

"I thought you said he was St. John's business partner?" Kilgor asked.

"He owns twenty percent of the company, but St. John runs the show. They're best friends and both were friends with the Mateo woman."

"I don't like this," Kilgor said, rubbing out his cigarette in the ashtray. "Not even a little."

●　　●　　●

Kilgor and the Colonel left Shaw and Alpine alone, arguing over how to deal with their problem.

Their arguing had gotten them nowhere except tired. "What will we tell Leon-Francis?" Victor asked.

Shaw scribbled in his planner. "Nothing. Once Travis is out of the way, we'll be fine."

"I hope you're right."

Shaw looked up. "Aren't I always? Look, this thing has gotten a lot bigger than either of us intended, but it's confinable. Just stay focused, Victor. Don't panic, and we'll be okay," he said, smiling. He went back to his writing.

Alpine was not as confident. He poured himself a fresh cup of coffee. "I'm not so sure about that."

Alpine's whimpering was beginning to irritate Shaw. "I've worked too hard and come too far to be worried about what anyone thinks."

Alpine fiddled with his cup, shaking he head without realizing it.

"You have to trust me. If it hadn't been for me, you'd still be a faceless Evergreen bureaucrat."

"Now and then I think how much happier my life was before I became mayor, and my ambition got the better of me."

Desmond Shaw quit writing and closed the planner. "Give me a break. You wanted this more than anyone. You have an opportunity to be one of the most powerful men in the world and you want to quibble about a few deaths. It's the price you pay for having power."

"Don't forget, I'm not like you," Alpine objected. "I've always envied your tenacity and the determination with which you go after what you want. And you always get it, no matter the cost. You would have made a great politician, if you cared about anything other than yourself. Your love of power and money outweighs your concern for people and principals. You equate power and fear with respect, but it isn't the same."

Shaw could no longer restrain his anger. "You have the nerve to lecture me about morals and decency, but where were your standards when you came to me for money because you needed a way around the campaign financing laws? Or when you whined about Eva Ward? I don't remember standards getting in the way when you asked for more money to pay off the little honey you knocked up. You're a hypocrite, Victor. The difference is, you think your noble ends justify your means and that they somehow make you different from me. They don't. The fact is, you and I are just alike. I accept who and what I am, while you want to continue living some fairy tale illusion. Now, can we get back to work?"

"You're despicable. I see now why Travis hates you so much."

Shaw straightened up slowly, towering over the shorter man. "What are you talking about?"

Alpine made an effort not to wince. "I know he's been blackmailing you for a long time. Whatever Dana has on you must be good. Why else would you keep him on the payroll all these years? What does he have that scares you so much? Kilgor and the Colonel may believe they're looking for bookkeeping records and some of the other garbage you feed them, but I know better."

"That's crazy." Shaw stuffed his planner into his briefcase and got up from the table to put on his coat.

"Is it?" Alpine sipped his coffee, watching him.

Shaw started to leave, full of fury, but thought better of it. "All right, Victor. Let's stop our bickering and finish the job. We're both on the verge of realizing our dreams. We can see the Promised Land; all we have to do is possess it. We can't let ourselves fall apart now, we're going to have to answer to Leon-Francis, and I don't think either of us wants that. What do you say?"

Alpine's silence despite his ugly scowl, served as a sign of agreement. Their unholy alliance had brought them too far for them to turn back now.

"Good, we need to decide on a contingency plan in case the Colonel's men can't deliver the goods."

"What if his men are caught? We can't afford to risk that.".

"I've been thinking about that too. The press is going to scrutinize every area of your life once you're elected. You can't afford to have any liabilities hanging around. I'm not worried about that slut you got pregnant ten years ago. She's being well paid and will keep her mouth shut, but Kilgor and the Colonel are another matter. People could accept you dallying around with a good-looking twenty-year-old. They won't, however, understand you associating with a psycho cop and a mercenary. They may decide they want more, particularly Kilgor. He's a loose cannon. The Colonel is more disciplined, but I can't trust him to keep his mouth shut forever, especially if his men go down."

"You're right; we may need to dispose of them when the time comes." Alpine was surprised how easily those words flowed from his mouth, and so was Shaw. The fact was, Alpine had never liked those two. They were constant reminders of how far he had fallen.

"Good, then we're in agreement for once," Shaw said, smiling.

"So how do we do it?"

"I already have that figured out." Shaw explained his plan.

When he was finished, Alpine nodded eagerly. He never ceased to be amazed by Shaw's ability to surprise him with the unexpected.

CHAPTER

Jansen Park was located in the middle of downtown Evergreen across the street from the performing arts center and Venture Citizens Bank Building. The park was a favorite for most downtown workers because it offered a tranquil alternative from the noisy and stressful office environment. During the summer, the city sponsored Concerts in the Park made the park even more popular.

Travis pulled into his usual parking space next to the park. The noonday sun was just breaking over the tall fir trees that shaded the outdoor amphitheater. Several people had already arrived with their lunches and were waiting for the band to start. Travis didn't care much for crowds, but he did enjoy the park's solitude.

He glanced across the street at the bank. Judging by the long line of people waiting at the teller counter, he could take his time eating his sandwich. He reached for the thermos on the passenger seat and poured a cup of coffee. After lunch, he'd go over and take care of his banking business like he did every payday.

Travis was reclined in the seat reading a newspaper when four middle-aged male cyclists arrived. They locked their bikes against the lamp post next to his car and headed into the park. He could hear them laughing as they gave each other high-fives over something that was said. Travis felt a twinge of envy.

The men were obviously friends, something Travis didn't have. The closest person to him was Desmond. At one time they were good friends, but looking back at it now, Travis could see that the bond was more a result of mutual survival than friendship. Now Desmond was his enemy. *I'll be dammed if I let him cheat me out of my money.* Travis tossed the newspaper on the floor and got out of the car.

◉　◉　◉

Detective Kilgor watched Travis on the security monitor as the cashier counted out two hundred dollars. Travis stuffed the money in his wallet and went over to the manager's desk. He signed the registry allowing him entrance to the safe deposit vault.

Kilgor swiveled the chair around to the other monitor that offered a closed feed of the vault. Travis opened his safety deposit box and pulled out a backpack. He closed the lid, shoved the box back into the vault, and left.

Kilgor jumped from his seat, slipped the security guard an envelope stuffed with cash, and raced downstairs. When he got to the lobby, Travis was nowhere to be found. Kilgor ran outside where his men were waiting in the van.

"Where is he?" the detective asked.

"He hasn't come out yet," said one of the men.

"That's impossible. How'd he get past us?"

"He couldn't have," the officer replied. He paused. "Could he?"

Kilgor went back into the bank.

◉　◉　◉

Travis's body was trembling as he hid in one of the restroom stalls planning his next move. How could he be so stupid and careless? He should have known Desmond was not going to let him out of his sight. What really made him angry was that he had led Shaw's men to the bank. Travis had seen two of the men lurking outside near the door when he came up from the vault. Now he was trapped and worse; he had what Desmond wanted in the backpack he carried. He wiped the film of perspiration from his face while thinking about his next move. Ten minutes later he was spotted on the overhead surveillance camera leaving the restroom.

      ●   ●   ●

"He's headed toward the office suites on the first floor, Kilgor said, walking quickly toward the hallway. "You," he said, pushing the man closets to him. "Go around outside to make sure he doesn't come out the other exit. Before he could bark out orders to the other man, an alarm sounded. Minutes later, a swarm of police cars arrived.

      ●   ●   ●

Two Evergreen police officers cordoned off the block.

Kilgor flashed his badge as he came out the bank. "Travis left through the emergency door in the bank," he said to the officers as he continued across the street to Travis's abandoned car.

The door was locked. Kilgor used a crowbar to break the window and then popped the door lock open, but he didn't find anything. Then he pried the trunk open, where he found a leather-bound book wedged under the spare tire. Even before he opened it, his gut told him that it was important.

      ●   ●   ●

Travis had the cab driver drop him in the alley behind his house, where he entered through the back door. He stuffed some clothes in his backpack, grabbed Marcus's business card off the dresser, and went to the garage. He pulled the dusty blue tarp off his vintage Corvair and started the engine.

Driving quickly to the airport, he parked in an underground garage, and then walked six blocks over to the Landover Hotel, where he registered under an assumed name, paying cash for the room. He was beginning to feel that his luck was running out. He stretched out on the queen-sized bed, trying to think of a way out of his dilemma. It was obvious that Shaw had no intention of paying him off, which meant they were going to kill him. The only insurance Travis had that might keep him alive was the information he was carrying. Parking at the airport might buy him some time to come up with a plan, but right now he didn't have any place to go or enough money to get there.

CHAPTER
18

Spoon cut his vacation short in St. Thomas because Maurice Beale wanted to see him. That was bad enough, but then his plane was late arriving in Baton Rouge on Wednesday. Beale had expected him hours ago. He took a taxi twenty miles out to the bar that was marooned in the marsh, smothered by Cypress trees.

The dilapidated shack of bleached white Cypress planks and rusted-tin roof was too isolated for most people, but it offered the quickest route to the New Orleans Star. The bar owner ran a boating service from the back on the pier. Spoon paid his fair and took the steps down to the water.

An old man holding a tattered white bible preached on the evils of gambling to the few people paying attention. Spoon made an obscene gesture to the man as he walked around him. "Mister, you're a fool if you think folks around here are going to give up gambling or gumbo." He crossed the rickety pier to the swamp boat. The boat skimmed across the stagnant water, dropping him off at the riverboat.

He walked up the back ramp of the riverboat, which was short cut to Beale's office. He heard shouting the moment he stepped on board. He stood outside the door listening to the ranting.

● ● ●

Beale slapped the man in the face. "Say one more word and I'll bust your head open!"

The blow knocked the man backward, his left foot tripping over the empty whiskey bottle spinning on the floor. He stumbled against the desk clutching his bookkeeping ledger to his chest.

His trembling fingers pushed his eyeglasses in place. He coughed trying to clear his throat. "Mr. Beale…there's nothing I can do at this point. The state wants their money and they want it by next week. If they don't get, they'll close down the casino. I've done the best I can do…"

Maurice picked up the baseball bat leaning against the desk and swung it as hard as he could at the man's chest. "I told you not to say another damn word!"

● ● ●

Spoon jumped back from the door when he heard the bat cracking ribs. The poor slob was the third bookkeeper Beale had gone through in as many years. Beale was certifiably crazy and Spoon knew this was not the right time to bring him more bad news. He slipped out the back.

CHAPTER

Marcus stood on the terrace overlooking the backyard patio and garden, watching the daylilies, roses, and English delphiniums bask in the morning sun. The impeccably manicured three-acre estate was protected by wrought iron fencing and gates. The entire estate was nestled in the middle of a nature preserve and greenbelt. A roman stone walkway led from the patio through the arbor down to the swimming pool and cabana.

Marcus saw Doc coming through the arbor. "Up here," he said, motioning Doc to join him.

Caitlin was eating breakfast on the lower patio that adjoined the master bedroom. She glanced up from her newspaper as Doc approached the house. "Good morning, Doc, you have a minute?"

Doc stepped up on the cantilevered steps leading to the patio sitting area framed in a white pergola. He saw his reflection in the hand-glazed Italian white tile floor. Dozens of clay pots filled with assorted blue, purple, and white perennials sat atop the stone wall that partially enclosed the patio. He ducked under the hanging Chinese Wisteria and joined her at the table.

Caitlin greeted him with a bright smile. "Have some breakfast?"

"No, thanks. But I think I'll try some of your tea."

Caitlin poured him a cup of the herbal lemon tea.

"I almost forgot how beautiful this place is," he said, looking up at the clustered fuchsias growing along the pergola.

"Thank you. You know you're welcome to stay here as long as you want." She handed him the newspaper. "There's a nice little blurb about Anna in there. Her funeral service was lovely."

"Yes it was," he said, glancing at the caption under her picture.

"I didn't know she had such a large family."

"Six brothers and four sisters, not to mention a half dozen or so aunts and uncles who couldn't make the trip from the Philippines. I'm going to miss her." He'd been shaken by the feelings and memories the funeral had evoked. So instead of remembering, he talked.

"She lived a few blocks from our house, but I didn't really get to know her until we were out of school. Once I went off to college in Oregon, we didn't see each other much. While I was in school, my father moved to Evergreen to pastor a new church where he met Olivia Ward. They married a few years later. At the time, her daughter, Eva, was living in Seattle finishing up her doctorate at Seattle University. When Anna left Quik, I asked Eva to take her in until she could get back on her feet. Eve got her enrolled in college and the rest is history."

His mouth felt uncomfortably dry. "Anna never came back to California, although she and Quik talked occasionally by telephone. I don't think she ever stopped loving him, but she knew their relationship would never work." Doc chuckled. "Quik always has a talent for picking good women and Anna was the best. Present company excluded, of course." He saluted her with his teacup.

Caitlin smiled. "Thanks. But he's still carrying around a lot of guilt because of the way he treated her." She spread some jelly on her toast.

"Yeah, I'm sure he does. Back in the day, when he was in the streets, Quik was the meanest man on earth. I always admired Anna for sticking with him as long as she did. The best thing she ever did for him was to leave, because he'd never have left Oakland if she'd stayed. He needed a life change, and running off to Austin seemed to do the trick. He worked hard and married you, which, by the way, was the smartest decision he ever made."

"Oh, that's sweet, Doc." She pecked him on the cheek.

"I mean it. You changed his life. I don't know how, but you did. I knew you were special when he called to tell me he was getting married. I couldn't imagine him falling in love, much less wanting to marry anyone. Of course, I got another shock when I met you, because I was expecting to see an African Nubian princess with braids, not a blond cheerleader from Texas."

Caitlin smiled. "I was never a cheerleader, and I'm not from Texas. I was born in Rhode Island."

"Rhode Island? Nobody is born in Rhode Island. People go there for a vacation, or pass through on the way to New York, but nobody is born there."

Caitlin started laughing. "Well, I was."

He shrugged. "If you say so. But by the time you and Marcus met, you were working for your father, right?"

"Actually, I met him at my brother's construction company, where I worked during the summer months while going to school. One day my father came by to see me and Marcus was with him."

"What did your father think of him?"

Smiling widely, she replied, "He loved him like a son. Marcus had a natural instinct for the business and more street smarts than a private detective. He loves this stuff--not just the excitement and intrigue, but also the business side. And I have to admit he's really good at it. He's definitely found his niche in life. Sometimes when he talks about his past, it's hard to believe he's the same person. I don't think he even understands the miraculous transformation he went through. He just accepts it and thanks God every night, which you *know* is hard for a man like him to do."

"Yeah, when I look at where he used to be, and where he is now, it's more than amazing. Quik's done well for himself."

Caitlin bit off a piece of toast and chewed slowly, watching him. "There wouldn't be an SJS Force if it hadn't been for you. Thanks for being such a good friend when Marcus needed one so badly."

Doc laughed. "You and Quik are family, you know that. So you don't have to thank me every time you see me, Caitlin."

"Okay, I won't bring it up ever again," she said, smiling. "But before I can do that I want to ask you something, and I'd like the truth. It won't make me think any less of you."

Doc was suddenly wary, but he didn't let it show. "I don't know if that's good or bad. What's on your mind?"

"Where did you get the $500,000 you invested in SJS?"

His eyes widened slightly. "Don't you think that's a little personal?"

"Yes, but I'm hoping you trust me enough to tell me."

Doc was about to give her a flippant response, but noticed the serious look on her face. "The money was mine to give, if that's what's bothering you. I cashed in the stock my father left me. The rest came from savings, which until two days ago was more than enough to tide me over. But now I don't know if I have a job when I get back home. I may have to ask you guys for a loan until I decide on my next career," he said, smiling, while reaching across to refill his teacup.

Caitlin dropped her fork on the table and looked at him in amazement.

"You okay?" Doc asked.

"Didn't Marcus tell you about the money?"

"What money?"

"The money you've been earning as a partner of the St. John-Sebasst Force. Marcus established an account with his broker years ago in your name. Every year he's deposited twenty-percent of the business's net income into the account."

Frowning, he muttered. "He didn't have to do that. I told you both—no strings."

She shook her head in irritation. "Don't be an idiot! He wanted to do it, and I encouraged him. Last time I checked you were worth about $17.4 million."

He froze. "Are you joking?"

"You know I don't joke about money."

"Shit!" he blurted without thinking. "Sorry about the language, but I wasn't exactly prepared for that."

She laughed.

Doc regained his composure. "Seventeen million, huh?" He sipped his tea. "Asha will be happy to hear that. She's tired of buying me dinner."

Marcus heard laughter and leaned over the terrace. "Hey down there! Doc, I need to see you when you can find time to break yourself free of my wife."

"We're talking, Marcus. He'll see you later," Caitlin yelled back.

"Watch out, Doc, inquiring minds want to know. She's going to pick your brains clean," Marcus said.

"Now, where were we?" Caitlin asked as she moved her chair closer. "How's life, Doc?"

He sighed. "What you really mean is how is my love life. It's fine. Next subject."

"Are you still with Asha?"

"Yes. Someday you'll have to meet her, assuming she continues to put up with me," he joked.

"Any wedding plans I should know about?"

"I've got some things to work out in my life before I even *think* about getting married."

"Well don't wait too long. Pretty soon that smooth, good-looking black face is going to start cracking like old vinyl. Whatever issues you've got can wait. If she's intelligent and beautiful, as I'm sure she is, she's not going to waste her life waiting on you to straighten out yours. She can help you with your problems. You just have to trust her. That's why God made women wise."

Doc turned to face her. "Caitlin, you're amazing. Do you normally walk up to strangers and ask them to bare their innermost soul to you, or am I just special?"

"You're special; you know that. Tell me what's really bothering you and don't feed me any crap about an inability to commit to a relationship. I know you better than that. You're always wearing a mask. I want to see the real you."

"I don't like talking about myself. Let's just say I've made some mistakes that I can't undo, and now I have to live with the consequences. End of story."

Caitlin released her hold on his arm. "I don't want to hear it. If this is about some guilt you've been harboring, get over it. There's not a person on this planet who doesn't regret something about their miserable existence. God knows Marcus and I do, but you know what? We both made it through and so can you. I don't need to tell you that, you already know it."

Doc was speechless; he had no idea what to say. Caitlin was as outspoken as an evangelical preacher at a revival, and just as blunt in telling the truth. She was Doc's self-appointed inquisitor and he knew she was going to be more relentless than any special prosecuting attorney.

"We've got all day," she said. "What's up?"

He raised his hands in surrender. "You would have made a great therapist."

She locked her blue eyes on his as though she was searching for the truth hidden deep in his soul. His attempt at humor did nothing to dissuade her from her mission. She took advantage of the silence.

"You know, my father once told me something I'll never forget. He said that the most important quality in a person is trust. Someone who is really trustworthy will never betray you or hurt you. Your pain will be their pain, your sorrow their sorrow. There is no obstacle or problem that can't be weathered if you have trust. It's a rare commodity, but if you meet someone you trust a hundred percent with your life, marry him. He'll be your best friend for life. That's why my dad respected Marcus so much, and that's why I married him. We both trust him with our lives. I also trust you, Doc, and I want you to trust me. I love you and I want to help."

Doc searched for the words, but nothing came out at first. No matter how hard he tried, he couldn't articulate what he felt. Caitlin touched his hand as he slowly began to tell his story.

❋　　❋　　❋

"Since I was a kid, I've been fascinated with history. It was more real to me than any dime-store novel or movie, because it was true and filled with colorful characters and events. I loved reading about some of the great empires that I discovered in the Bible: Assyria, Babylon, and Rome. I soon began to see America as a great empire like the others, and there wasn't anything I wanted more than to be a soldier of that empire. 'Truth, justice and the American way,' was more to me than just a silly comic book motto. I wanted to live it.

"It didn't matter that my father wanted me to use my God-given talents for the ministry. I had other plans. I had my pick of jobs when I got out of school. I worked at the Department of Justice for a brief time before I got the job I really wanted, which was with the Secret Service."

"You guarded the president?" Caitlin didn't know why she was so surprised by the idea.

"No, they assigned me overseas to protect traveling American diplomats."

"No wonder we could never reach you. Why didn't you ever tell us?"

He looked apologetic. "I was stationed in so many countries that I eventually lost count. The diplomats and heads-of-state I worked for became an endless blur of faceless people, whose names I don't even remember. I believed in what I was doing and forgot the things that really mattered, like my friends and family. I was so absorbed with my own life, that I convinced myself I didn't have time to attend my own stepmother's funeral. When her daughter, Eva, disappeared, I convinced myself again that family wasn't as important as my career. I told Dad he didn't need me with him; the police would find out what happened and everything would be okay." He paused. "But it wasn't."

Caitlin leaned forward. "You can't blame yourself for what happened to Eva."

"Maybe if I'd paid more attention, if I had been around more, I would have seen something was wrong. Maybe I could have stopped it. Her death made me realize a lot of things. The Evergreen Police Department went through the pretense of an investigation, but that's all it was. They didn't care about truth, because someone had already bought that. They called that justice. And I wasn't any better. My father pleaded with me to stay, but I left Evergreen two days after arriving. After that, we didn't speak until his death." He stopped to take a breath. It felt odd to release all the words he had held captive inside for so long.

Caitlin's sympathetic expression never wavered.

"Over the next couple of years," Doc continued, "I provided security to forty-one diplomats and their families, and I never lost one. I was proud of that. It didn't matter that some of them were no better than the ones trying to kill them. I never let my personal feelings get in the way of doing my job, until I met Bryce Pettiborn.

"He was an Undersecretary of Commerce attending an international trade conference in Barcelona. I was assigned to protect him. He also brought six men of his own and it didn't take long to figure out why; he needed them to clean up after him. He was more interested in partying than in attending the conference. Every morning he woke up with a different woman in his bed, all of them with ominous bruises. One morning I heard a woman screaming from his suite. I raced down the hall to find a young woman was sitting in the middle of the floor—half naked. She was a Cuban model—at least she had been.

"She was looking at her reflection in the shattered mirror. Her lips were lacerated, her nose was broken, and her eyes were dark and swollen. Pettiborn's men were trying to get her dressed, while he sat in bed, smoking a cigarette and reading the paper as though nothing had happened. I wanted to kill him, but I left the room, determined that wouldn't happen again on my watch.

"On his last night in Portugal, I was passing his room when I heard crying and the sound of cracking bone. I kicked in the door and saw Pettiborn straddling a very young Portuguese girl—maybe twelve; his fist buried halfway in her face. I knocked him off her.

"He started swearing like a wild man. I slugged him again just as his men came in the door. They drew their guns and told me to back off. Pettiborn went crazy. He started kicking the girl, trying to get her to stop crying, but the fool couldn't see she was in shock. I slammed my gun into his face, but he kept going at her. I don't know who fired the first shot, but when it was over, Pettiborn and one of his men were dead. The girl died a day later of head trauma."

Caitlin was pale, but she waited in silence.

"The government never told Pettiborn's family the truth about what happened. He became another martyr who had given his life for his country. I wasn't that fortunate. They reassigned me to Washington, pending a full investigation.

"The panel wasn't interested in truth or justice. They should have sent an apology of regret to that little girl's family. Instead, they were only interested in finding out how I could shoot and kill the man I'd been sent to protect, as well as a loyal American soldier. It didn't matter that he'd been helping Pettiborn break the law, and violate the human rights of non-Americans, and that he'd been an accomplice to rape and murder. They said I should have simply walked away." He closed his eyes, clearly upset, trying to push his anger back down inside him, where it belonged.

"I was reprimanded and given a desk job working at the Treasury Building. About a year later I was coming home from work and stopped to pick up some food. Someone took a shot at me from the alley across the street. I returned the fire. When I went to investigate, I found the body of a boy. Later that night, I learned he was Pettiborn's oldest son. I suspect some government bureaucrat leaked the truth to the family." Doc ran his hand restlessly over his shiny head as if to smooth away the memory.

"I was glad Bryce Pettiborn was dead. I knew I'd done the right thing, but killing his son was different. He was only fifteen; he didn't deserve to die. A night doesn't pass that I don't think about him. I started hating myself for what I'd become, and I hated the government for their part in it.

"Shortly afterwards, my father got sick. I was fortunate to make it home before he died. On his deathbed he forgave me for all those times I wasn't there for him and the family. His only request of me was to get it right with God. He told me how proud he had always been of me. Then he kissed me and died."

Caitlin held his hand and gave him a reassuring smile. "I wish I had met your father. He sounds like he was a remarkable man."

All that talking had made his mouth dry—at least he thought it was the talking. Perhaps it was something else. "He was the best man I've ever known. After I buried him, I no longer had a desire to serve my country. They had already taken enough from me. I left the Service and never looked back. I made up my mind I was going to make a change in my life, and that's what I've been doing these last six years. The only thing I want from the government now is for them to clear my name. My attorneys are working on it now. Other than that, I'm just trying to get my head straight so I can finish the race."

Caitlin considered carefully before she said, "That's the very reason you need a woman in your life. Asha can help you begin to heal. You may never be whole again, but by expressing your feelings and thoughts to someone you trust, you can cope with them a little easier."

"I'm not sure I want to cope with it." He was surprised by the exclamation, but she wasn't.

"Doc, life is pain; you can't avoid it. Pettiborn's son made a stupid choice that unfortunately got him killed, but you're not to blame. He paid the consequence for making the wrong decision."

Doc looked at her with new respect. She told the cold hard truth without sugarcoating. There was no condemnation or rejection in her voice, just the blunt statement of the facts. "The thing is, I'm not sure I'm ready to talk about this with anyone else, *especially* Asha."

"You have to. You'll feel better about it, trust me. Your indiscretions pale in comparison to Marcus's experiences, but he was smart enough to marry a wise woman like me, and I'm there to help him through the tough times. Asha can do the same for you."

Doc got up abruptly. "That reminds me, I need to call her."

"The phone is right there on the table."

"I'll call a little later, after I find out what your husband is so anxious to discuss with me."

Caitlin frowned. "What's going on?"

"What do you mean?" His mask was back in place.

"I'm not stupid. I know you and Marcus are up to something. Every time I turn around, you're meeting with him and Max. He's not telling me much, other than that he's looking into Anna's death. Don't let him do anything crazy. I'm too young to be a widow and he's too old for jail." She said it lightly, but her blue eyes were dark and serious.

"Don't worry about Quik. He'll be okay."

Caitlin knew he was lying. She thought of pressing him for the truth, but decided against it. Maybe she was better off not knowing.

Before she could speak again, Doc leaned over and kissed her. "Thanks

CHAPTER

The corporate home of the Shaw Development Company was a marble office building overlooking the bay in Evergreen. Shaw sat in his office suite on the top floor, looking out the window, down at the boardwalk. It was late afternoon, the sun was still hot, and the pier was crowded with people taking advantage of the nice weather.

Shaw's secretary suddenly opened the door. "Sorry to disturb you, Mr. Shaw, but you wanted to go over your schedule?"

"Come on in. What time is my meeting with Public Works?"

"They cancelled because one of the commissioners couldn't make it. They want to reschedule for next week."

"Next week is fine, but I'm tired of them jerkin' me around. Reschedule the meeting for a half-hour instead of one hour. I don't need their approval to go ahead with the project. What's next?"

"Mayor Alpine's press conference at 5:00. Your tailor needs fifteen minutes to fit your new suit, and you have to leave here by 6:15 for the fundraiser. On her way out of the office she said, "Oh, you wanted me to remind you about the mayor's speech tonight."

"Yes, thanks. Cancel the rest of my appointments and please order me some lunch." Shaw sat at his desk and turned the computer monitor on. Alpine's speech was there, waiting for him to finish it. Writing the speeches had become second nature to him, and boring. The fact was, Victor Alpine was his creation. He had created the persona, honed his skills, and told him what and how to think. Shaw had a gift for transforming the ordinary into something great. Alpine had possessed two innate qualities that made him a good leader: he was likable and charismatic. Shaw's job was to remove his tarnish, polish him up, and make him electable.

Shaw finished the last few pages of Alpine's speech and sent it to the printer. It was filled with the same rhetoric and promises of former speeches, but it didn't really matter. Alpine would easily win the election over his Democratic opponent—an inexperienced lawyer with enough personal baggage to keep the tabloids in business for a year.

Shaw placed the speech in his briefcase, and then found himself staring out the window again, but this time, at nothing in particular. He unconsciously pulled out the silver and gold key he always kept in his vest pocket and thought about his future. He had come a long way since his inauspicious beginnings in Massachusetts, where he'd left a life he never wanted to remember. The bad memories of Boston had now been replaced with good thoughts. Shaw flipped the key over in his hand. Soon, he would have more money than he would be able to spend in a lifetime, but as satisfying as that was, it couldn't compete with power. Once Alpine was in the White House, he would owe Shaw for everything, and the price would be hefty.

Shaw heard noise coming from the private conference room. He opened the double doors and saw Kilgor and the Colonel pouring themselves coffee. "What are you two doing here?"

"Relax, no one saw us enter. We used the private door," Kilgor said.

"We weren't supposed to meet until later this evening, after the fundraiser. What's so important?"

"We couldn't wait until tonight. What are you pulling, Shaw?" Kilgor demanded.

"What are you talking about?"

The Colonel stepped forward. "You damn well know what we're talking about. You've been lying to us about Travis. He doesn't have anything on us."

Shaw was puzzled. "Of course he does."

"I don't think so," the Colonel said lazily. Travis didn't leave any records or files at the bank, but we found this hidden in the trunk of his car."

Kilgor flung the brown book on the table.

Shaw looked at it cautiously before touching it. "What's in it?"

"Look for yourself," Kilgor said.

Reluctantly, Shaw opened the book and turned to the paper clipped pages. His face turned red and his mouth went dry.

"You've been telling us for weeks that Travis had us over a barrel because of some piss-ass financial records he stole. You didn't say anything about *this*. He says in that diary of his that you paid some guy to whack his father. I don't suppose that was the real reason he's been hounding you?" Kilgor asked.

Shaw's face went from red to pale, revealing the anger and embarrassment he felt. He tossed the diary back on the table. "Yes, I admit, I've been somewhat less than candid with you but I had my reasons. How would it look if Victor Alpine's campaign manager were involved in a murder scandal on the eve of his greatest victory? We've come too far to be shot down by a scandal. Anyway, I wasn't lying. Travis does have his hands on some very sensitive documents that can send all of us to prison for a very long time. There's no way I'd pay that creep one dollar, much less the $3 million he's asking. And now you can see why. That devious bastard is crazy and liable to do anything."

"Does Victor know about any of this?" Kilgor asked.

"He knows only what I want him to know, and that's the way it's going to stay. Look, I'm sorry I stretched the truth, but this wasn't something I wanted to tell the world about. Travis always blamed me for his father's accident; that's all it is. Now, I pay you both good money to do what I tell you to do, and you'll make even more once Victor is elected. We just have to stop Travis."

"That may be a problem now," Kilgor said.

"Why?"

Kilgor shifted uncomfortably. "He's gone. He showed up at the bank like you said, but escaped with a backpack of stuff he had in his safe deposit box. We got our people out looking for him."

"Did you check his house?"

"Of course we did." The detective seemed affronted. "It's the first place we went. He packed up a few things and took his Corvair. I've got people all over the city looking for him."

Shaw paced the floor, trying to think. "He may be running. If he is, he won't get far in that car. You better station some men at the train depot and bus station. He's got a phobia about flying, but send a few people out to the airport, just in case."

"His car should be easy enough to find," Kilgor assured him with false bravado. "I'll contact the state troopers. We'll get it done."

Shaw turned to the Colonel, who had been oddly silent throughout the exchange. "What progress are your people in California making?"

"They're ready to go," the Colonel replied slowly. "Sebasst and St. John will be history by this time tomorrow," he said confidently.

"How many men have you got?" Kilgor asked.

"Ten. More than enough to handle the situation if something goes wrong."

"Good. I want to enjoy my dinner tomorrow when I see the governor. Knowing these guys are out of the way will make my food go down easier," Shaw said.

Chapter

Sydney Belleshota usually combined a security sweep of the grounds with her daily four mile run. Today, she cut her run short, returning to the house through the back gate instead of the front.

"That was quick," Caitlin said as Sydney came into the kitchen.

"It's probably just as well you didn't go with me. My leg started cramping halfway around the lake."

"Maybe I'll go tomorrow," Caitlin said. "I can't seem to pry Marcus away from Doc long enough for him to go jogging with me."

"Speaking of your husband, where is he?"

"Upstairs on the terrace with Doc and Max. If you're going up, remind him we have to leave for the city by two for the girls to go to the movies."

"Okay," Sydney plucked an orange from the fruit basket before heading up the stairs to the terrace.

Marcus and Max sat at an inlaid marble table, while Doc relaxed on the chaise lounge.

"What have you found out so far?" Marcus asked Max.

"Alpine has been mayor of Evergreen for over eight years. He has a pretty impressive record: revolutionized and privatized the city's social service programs and transit system, and single-handedly revitalized the city's downtown district. He's a skilled negotiator too. He knows how to use his power."

"What about family?" Marcus asked.

"Not much is going on in his personal life. His wife died years ago from cancer. He never remarried or had kids. Prior to being mayor, he served as Evergreen's Planning Commissioner for fifteen years. He's a fiscal conservative and social moderate. The Republicans didn't think much of him until he won the primary last Tuesday. Now they're licking his boots and hailing him as the next savior. He has a powerful political machine that's supported in large part by out-of-state interests. If he's receiving illegal campaign contributions, there's no smoking gun. The state Attorney General's Office recently completed a year long ethics probe. Several politicians were found to have violated campaign finance laws in varying degrees, but Alpine was completely exonerated. So far, I can't find any dirt on him."

Doc and Marcus exchanged glances. That was very disappointing. They'd been hoping for more.

"However, I can't say the same for Desmond Shaw. His family background is sketchy. He was raised in Norfolk, Virginia. His mother abandoned him at an early age and he was raised by an abusive father. He ran away when he was thirteen and lived on the streets for awhile before being be-friended by a youth counselor who placed him with foster parents. Evidently he thrived in that environment, because the parents mortgaged their house to send him to school at MIT. I guess he's some kind of math whiz." Max took another sip of his apple juice. "Anyway, the father lost his job and house, and Shaw dropped out of school to help support the family. A year later he got caught running a Ponzi scam out of a frat house."

"What was the scam?" Marcus asked.

"Commodity trading. He convinced a businessman to invest $50,000, guaranteeing him a twenty percent return on investment in thirty days. One month later, Shaw paid the man back his fifty grand, plus the $10,000 he'd promised. After six months, Shaw and his partners had so much money coming in they stopped taking on new investors—and that was the beginning of the end. Ponzi schemes rely on the constant infusion of new money to work. When Shaw couldn't repay his initial investor's $700,000, the financial pyramid fell apart. Shaw and three frat brothers were charged with fraud. Everyone but Shaw served time. In fact, he was never convicted."

"How did that happen?" Doc asked.

"His primary investor accidentally died eight months before the trial—and so did half of the state's case against Shaw. His high-priced lawyer did the rest by getting the case dismissed on a series of procedural technicalities."

Max removed his horned-rimmed glasses and massaged the bridge of his nose before putting them back on. "Now, this is where the story gets interesting. The major investor bankrolling Shaw--the one who lost the most money in the scam--was a real estate broker named Calvin Henry Travis. Dana Travis's father. A little more digging and I found that Travis and Shaw are first cousins."

Marcus shot up out of the chair. "Cousins!"

"Yep, Shaw and Travis's mothers were sisters. Travis's mother died with his dad while vacationing in Sun Valley. Supposedly they lost control of their snowmobile and plunged into a ravine. Travis's sister suspected foul play, but could never prove anything."

"Where was Travis at the time?" Sydney asked.

"He was estranged from the family and working for one of the big accounting firms in Boston. Eventually he was fired for playing around with client accounts. A few months later, Desmond Shaw formed a real estate company, moved to Evergreen and hired Travis as his accountant."

Max leaned his elbows on the table and continued, aware that everyone was waiting anxiously. "I spoke with Travis's sister and she says he would do anything for a buck. That's why his father disinherited him in his will, leaving the daughter everything. She's always believed Desmond Shaw had her parent's killed, and that Travis was somehow involved. The bottom line here: Shaw is far more dangerous than we thought. He's the real mover and shaker, and the power behind Alpine. He runs the political machine that keeps the man in office, and uses two thugs--Lane Kilgor and an ex-Army Colonel named Thaddeus Grier--to enforce his will." Max poured himself some more juice. "I think we've been duped by Travis; this whole mess seems to be about blackmail."

"If that's all Travis has on him, Shaw could have killed him years ago," Doc offered.

Sydney leaned against the terrace rail, eating her orange and listening closely. It didn't matter who was right; either way they were in a lot of trouble. She finished the last slice of orange before pulling a bronzed projectile from her pocket and tossing it on the table. It bounced off the table top onto Max's lap. "I found it this morning."

"What's this?" Max asked.

"A rifle cartridge."

"Let me see that," Doc said. Max handed him the shell. Doc inspected it carefully like a surgeon reviewing x-rays. "Where exactly did you get this?"

"On the back trail between the house and the south gate," Sydney replied.

"Show me." Doc's forehead was furrowed and he spoke softly— too softly.

Sydney pointed to a cluster of trees off to the left. "On the other side of the iron fencing there's a trail that runs through the woods over to the back road by the gate. The cartridge wasn't there Monday morning, and the gate was closed for the funeral yesterday."

"What's the road used for?" Doc persisted.

"Deliveries, maintenance and gardening folks, mostly," Max told him.

Doc handed the cartridge back to Sydney "M-80?"

"Yeah, and none of our people use sniper rifles," she said.

"What the hell is going on here?" Marcus demanded. But he knew the answer—part of it, anyway.

"Someone was in the woods Monday or Tuesday night, watching you and, judging from where I found that cartridge, I'd say they picked the perfect spot for spying on your study. It's about one hundred and fifty yards to the house. At that range, this bullet could've taken off your head. The grounds have to be secured immediately. I'm putting men everywhere around the house and on the gates," Sydney said.

"You're talking about half a dozen men. That won't work. Caitlin will know that something is up."

Sydney loosened a piece of orange peel stuck between her teeth. "We'll need more than six. As far as Caitlin, either tell her what's up or get her and your kids out of here until we know it's safe."

"It's still not too late to go to the police," Max said weakly.

"Out of the question," Marcus said. He turned to Doc. "What do you think?"

"I agree with Sydney. You need protection, *now*. Get Caitlin and the kids out of the house tonight, if not sooner. Whoever these guys are, they're professionals, and they'll probably be back."

"If you're right about this, why didn't they take their shot when they had it?" Marcus asked.

Doc thought for a moment. "They saw or heard something they didn't like."

"Mondays are our heaviest delivery days. We didn't get back from Seattle until late Monday afternoon. It would have been easy enough for someone to sneak onto the grounds," Sydney pointed out.

"She may be right." Doc was suddenly on his feet. "I'd check for wiretaps."

Marcus refused to believe it. "That's impossible. These guys couldn't have pulled all this together so fast."

"With enough money, you can do anything," Sydney said.

"We have a bigger problem now." Doc crossed his arms. "Shaw and Alpine may know our plans. And if they do, they'll be waiting for me in Evergreen, and Leon-Francis will have a big surprise for you if you set foot in San Diego."

CHAPTER

Later that evening, Victor Alpine and Desmond Shaw rode in a black stretch limousine with the state Speaker-of-the-House, Mary Simms, and Charles Onger, chairman of the state Republican Party.

"That was a great speech you gave tonight, Victor. The press was out in full force and you made one hell of an impression on them. The positive press coverage should push you a couple of percentage points," Onger said with great enthusiasm.

Mary Simms raised a hand as if to quell him. "That's true, but it's also true that your opponent is stepping up her campaign and sources say she's ready to go on the offensive. She's mounting an all-out media campaign against you. They're going to attack your support of the Claiborne Bill and your stand against abortion. She's getting ready to play hardball and we could slip a bit. As your campaign finance manager, I can tell you we may need more money to keep on the offensive. The Democrats are throwing all their weight behind her. They don't intend to lose this seat."

"Don't worry about the money, Mary, we'll get whatever you need," Alpine said.

Simms and Onger glanced at each other and then to Desmond

Shaw, whose smile was the only confirmation they needed. Both knew the rules of the game. Never ask where the money comes from; that way you can remain blissfully ignorant. The telephone rang. "Desmond Shaw."

"This is Kilgor. We found his car at one of the airport garages."

"Has he left town?"

"I don't think so. A parking attendant saw him park the Corvair and hop on a hotel shuttle bus going to the strip. He's likely hiding out in one of them. We're checking them now. We'll have him by morning."

"That's great. Make sure you have a welcome party to show him how much we appreciate all he's done." Shaw hung up the phone.

"Another contributor with a donation?" Mary asked.

"Yes, you could say that. We've been after him for a while and now it appears he's ready to commit a substantial amount to Victor's campaign."

"Oh, I would like to meet him."

"It will have to wait. His time is limited and I'm afraid he won't be around after tomorrow."

●　　●　　●

Fear kept Travis confined to his hotel room. When he finally got to sleep, a nightmare woke him at 3:20. He was drenched in sweat.

He jumped out of bed and put on his pants as he peered through the sheer drapes. The streets were empty, but intuition told him Shaw's men were close. He slipped on a clean shirt and his shoes. For a moment he sat motionless on the side of the bed, trying to come up with a plan. He cursed himself for being so stupid. If they found his car, and he suspected they had, the strip would be crawling with guys looking for him.

Travis splashed water on his face and packed his backpack. Then he checked to make sure the hallway was clear. He decided against taking the elevator. Instead, he took the stairs down to the lobby. The foyer was empty, except for the young man working at the registration desk. Travis crossed the room to the large window facing the street. Three men sat in a Monte Carlo across the street. Two of them appeared to be sleeping, while the third man was lighting a cigarette.

Sweat formed on his forehead again. He ran down the steps to the garage and out the door to the side street. A homeless man stared at him as he hugged the garage wall, inching his way to the corner of the building. The car was still parked at the curb. The driver suddenly turned around and Travis thought he had been spotted, but the man was just passing his thermos to the two men in the back seat, who were now awake. Travis crept back behind the cover of the hotel, turned and ran as fast as his penguin body would take him in the opposite direction.

CHAPTER

The New Orleans Star had been one of the finest riverboat casinos on the Mississippi. The Star was a replica of a 1860s side-wheel paddleboat that could comfortably accommodate 1,700 guests on three gaming decks. It had been the most profitable casino on the Mississippi and a major tourist attraction until falling on hard times under Maurice Beale's mismanagement.

Beale had been napping on the couch before the nightmare woke him up screaming. It happened often, especially when he dreamt of her. His hand still clutched the baseball bat lying next to him on the couch. One of his men knocked on the door to make sure he was okay. His men where smart enough to keep their distance from him when he was in one of his "moods" as Beale referred to them.

Beale rolled off the couch and stood up. His head felt like it was on fire. He staggered to his desk looking for some whiskey to quench his pain, where he found some rotgut sherry buried underneath a layer of invoices and unpaid bills. Beale shot his arm across the desk, sweeping everything off his desk. "I ain't paying nobody!" It was that kind of irrational thinking that made him so dangerous and unpredictable—as his bookkeeper discovered earlier.

Everyone that worked for Maurice Beale knew he detested bad news, especially if it concerned money. He was a man void of any integrity, with loyalty to none. He would steal a penny from a kid if he left it on the table too long.

Beale stood in his office staring at the stream of people entering the casino on the portside promenade deck. His mind was elsewhere. The French Creole sported an outdated goatee and ponytail, which he had a habit of twisting. A day didn't go by that he didn't think about her.

He once had a promising career in the Sampa crime family, but that had long since disappeared, along with his wife, Ezea. She was the one he blamed for most of his misfortunes, and the person responsible for his uncontrollable rage.

* * *

Ezea Sheppard was a naïve seventeen-year-old working in her aunt's restaurant when Beale first met her. She had already acquired the beauty and grace of a mature woman, and her jade eyes made her a popular model. Beale fell in love with her the first time he met her. She delivered sandwiches in New Orleans to local businesses in the French Quarter. Beale was almost twice her age, but that didn't stop him from becoming obsessed with her. He showered her in flowers and expensive gifts. It took a year for him to convince her that a life spent with him was much preferable to living with her exploitive aunt.

The honeymoon was hardly over before Beale's gambling house business at the casino took a nosedive, and so did the marriage. He had kept a lid on his behavior for almost two years, but like a lion returning to the fight, the madness came roaring back. It started with temper tantrums when dinner wasn't prepared on time or when she wasn't home when he got there: small things. It escalated when he complained about the way she cleaned the house, or the way she did her hair, or ironed his shirts. By the fourth year, the psychosis was in high gear.

Ezea was subjected to constant beatings over imagined affairs and liaisons with men she never knew. The worse business got, the more her husband found a reason to hit her. He beat her when he thought she looked too good, and he beat her if she didn't look good enough.

Ezea tried leaving him several times, but he always found her and dragged her back home. One night after losing a lot of money gambling, he savagely beat her with a razor strap, leaving a permanent six-inch whelp on her neck. A few months later, on their fifth wedding anniversary, she prepared a romantic candlelight dinner, and served him his favorite brandy. The brandy was laced with enough codeine to knock out a horse.

Once he was asleep, she took a crowbar, broke into his wall safe, and stole the $23,500 Beale owed Tippi Sampa. The next morning Beale found a note dangling from the hole in the wall that read: "Happy Anniversary."

Beale rubbed the stubs of his missing right index and forefinger, which were constant reminders of her deceit. It was the price he'd paid when he was unable to give the Sampas their money. The fact that it was his wife who'd ripped him off made the humiliation even worse. After that, Tippi Sampa exiled him to the Star to watch over their interests.

Although he was listed as the owner/manager of the casino, he had no real authority to do anything. He was just the front man who legitimized the operations. The Sampas skimmed so much off the profits, Beale could barely stay a step ahead of the IRS and Louisiana Revenue Department. Things only got worse after Leon-Francis took over Sampa's operations, including the riverboat. Maurice was allowed to stay on as manager, but at a greater cost. He had to pay Leon-Francis thirty-five percent of the profits.

●　●　●

When Spoon entered the office, Beale was sitting at his desk sharpening his knife.

"It's about time you showed up," Beale said.

"Sorry about that. I had some trouble. The plane got here late," Spoon said.

Beale grunted as he checked the sharpness of the knife blade with his finger. "So, are you sure it was my wife you saw in St. Thomas?"

"Yeah, I've seen these pictures a hundred times," he said, caressing the photo on Beale's desk.

"Those pictures are old, people change. How can you be sure it's her?"

"No one has damn eyes like hers, and she still looks a lot like this."

Beale looked up.

Spoon forgot he was still holding the picture. Embarrassed that he had been caught lusting over his employer's wife, he placed the frame gently back on the desk. "She's changed her name, but I'm telling you, boss, it's her. I even saw the scar on her neck. Her hair is shorter, but it's her. I'd know her anywhere."

"I bet you would."

Beale stared at him and Spoon felt a bead of perspiration forming on his temple. His boss was slight in stature, but was still big enough to make people disappear.

"What do you want me to do?" Spoon asked.

"Whatever I tell you, you better do it with your brains. If you so much as look at my wife out of the corner of your eye, you'll wish you had been born a woman. Now, tell me what else you found out."

Spoon released a quiet sigh of relief and stole another peek at the photo. "She's doing real well for herself. Got a fancy restaurant and nice home on the Islands. From all indications, she's got plenty of dough, too. She's made some large endowments to the local university."

"How does she look?"

Spoon searched for the right words. "She's still beautiful, just older."

Beale had never loved a woman like he loved Ezea. She kept him as close to center as he would ever get. When he lost her, he lost everything he had—his business, status, money and dreams. His diseased mind could still recall her scent and every detail of her curvaceous body. The haunting vision of her visited him every night while he was sleeping, only to disappear when he tried to reach out and touch her. The thought of another man enjoying her flesh was the ultimate transgression, and made him lose all sense of reality. "Is she married?"

"No, but she's been with the same guy for a couple of years, a professor at the university. Seems like they're pretty tight."

That sent a visible shudder through Beale's body. A smirk formed at the corners of Spoon's lips. He decided to twist the knife a little more. "Yeah, a couple of people at her restaurant told me this is the only guy she's been serious about. I think they live together." That got another rise from him.

The look of rage on Beale's face was undeniable. He had spent the better part of seventeen years searching for her. He never once thought of giving up. The hate ran too deep, and now fate had allowed another chance. He had waited a long time for this.

She would suffer as he had, eye for eye and measure for measure. She would know what it meant to lose everything dear to her, just like he knew.

Beale closed his switchblade and put it back in his pocket. He opened his center desk drawer, pulling out a stash of cash and airline tickets. He threw the money at Spoon. "I want you and the boys at the airport by midnight. We're going hunting.

CHAPTER

Marcus watched his wife from the guesthouse window as she picked a bouquet of flowers from the garden. He had made up some flimsy excuse for not going with her and the kids to the movies. While they were gone, he had the house and property swept for bugs. Sydney found two attached beneath the terrace, one on the patio outside his bedroom, and one under the limousine. Knowing that someone had gotten that close to his family only made him angrier. The pounding of new siding being nailed to the guesthouse finally drove him outside. He ducked under the scaffolding and saw Doc and Sydney talking by the pool.

"Is the house clean yet?" Marcus asked.

"I think so," Sydney replied. "We found another bug in the study, but I want to sweep it again, just to make sure. For the time being, I think we should stay in the guesthouse and only use cell phones until we're absolutely sure."

"How about security?"

"I've got seven men covering the woods and roads. The rest are stationed on the grounds and in the house. What about Caitlin?"

"She and the kids are going to stay at one of the downtown hotels for a couple of days. If things start to get hot, I'll send them to her father in Vegas."

Sydney nodded. "So what's the next move?"

Raising his eyebrows as if it were obvious, Marcus told her, "We have to find Travis as soon as possible, if he's still alive."

"That's going to be tough. They're expecting you," she said.

"Good. That means I won't have to go far to find them."

Sydney was not impressed. "That's not exactly logical."

"I don't care. I'm going to get these bastards before they get me."

"Then we're going to have to be discreet. You can't fly that giant Gulfstream of yours into Seattle/Tacoma without being noticed," Doc pointed out.

Marcus crossed his arm. "So give me some options."

"I have a friend who works security at Boeing Airfield. I'll see if we can get clearance to land there," Doc said.

"What do we do if we can't find Travis?" Sydney asked.

"We have to find the files he had on him," Marcus said.

"That makes sense." Doc folded the newspaper he was reading and laid it on the table. "But if you show yourself in Evergreen, you're likely to run into something worse than just Shaw and Alpine."

"If you're talking about Leon-Francis, I'm not convinced he's involved in any of this," Marcus said.

"You're kidding."

"No, I'm not. They made a mistake by not taking out Travis. Leon-Francis doesn't make mistakes. He would have killed Travis from the get-go, and whacked our asses for extra measure."

"For our sake, I hope you're right," Doc said.

CHAPTER

Travis was on the run all night, resting little and avoiding cars when possible. He traveled through wooded residential neighborhoods and back streets. By morning, he found himself catching his breath behind a furniture distribution center, eight miles west of the airport. A white Monte Carlo sat at the corner, waiting its turn to pull into the parking lot.

The hairs on Travis's neck stood on end. Quickly, scrambling and breathing hard, he found a place to hide in a small crawl space behind a stack of pallets. The car slowly circled the building, but quickly sped off when the driver found the lot empty. Travis tried to stand up, but his arthritic leg wouldn't let him. He toppled back to the ground, clutching his knee. Even if he could walk, he didn't have any place to go. And he was tired—bone tired. He rested his head on a pallet and, despite the rigid discomfort, closed his eyes.

Three hours later, he woke, heart racing, to the noise of a sputtering forklift. It attacked a pile of pallets next to him, lifting and moving them back into the warehouse. Travis struggled to his feet. Sleeping in the cramped space had worsened his knee and now he could barely walk, much less run. One of the large bay doors of the warehouse opened and a truck pulled out. The driver opened the rear doors, and went back into the warehouse. Moments later, workers began moving furniture into the transport truck.

Travis watched, eyes narrowed, as he tried to control his breathing and erratic heartbeat. Finally, he hobbled alongside the truck and jumped in the back when the men weren't looking. Ten minutes later the doors swung shut and the truck eased out of the parking lot. Travis stretched his leg out on a plastic-covered couch pushed against the wall. He didn't have a clue where he was going and he didn't care as long as it was taking him away from Desmond Shaw. There was solace in the darkness, and for the first time in twenty-four hours, he felt safe.

Forty minutes later the truck stopped and Travis hid behind the couch. The doors swung open and the driver started unloading furniture. On the second trip, Travis sneaked out and found himself standing in the middle of a new housing development called Summerfield. He looked around frantically to see where he was, half expecting to see a sign reading "Another Development by Desmond Shaw." Instead, he found a banner; it seemed AudPlaza Properties owned the place. He had no idea where he was.

"Good morning, may I help you?" asked a woman who suddenly appeared out of nowhere.

Travis flinched. *Where had she come from?* He had to think fast. "I was in the neighborhood and thought I'd take a look at your model townhouses." He hoped she couldn't hear the quiver in his voice.

Apparently she didn't. She introduced herself, and he told her his name was Johnson.

"I'd be happy to give you a tour. As you can see, we're still in the process of furnishing some of the models. Did you have a particular model in mind?"

"Perhaps a two-bedroom or three-bedroom unit. What size is this?" he asked as they walked toward the office.

"This is our deluxe three-bedroom model, which we've temporarily converted into our sales office. It comes equipped with…"

Travis smiled attentively, though he barely heard a word of her sales pitch. While she rambled on, he studied the map on the wall behind her desk. Based on the colorful pushpins representing the subdivision on the map, Travis figured Summerfield was somewhere in South Seattle—only a few miles from where he'd started.

"That's just great," he mumbled.

"Excuse me; did you say something, Mr. Johnson?"

"No, just talking to myself."

Travis didn't have transportation or any idea of what to do next, so he decided to stay in Summerfield until he had a plan. He took a tour of the houses with the agent and took advantage of the free food and refreshments. By then he was limping more noticeably, and his breathing was labored. Not to mention that his nerves were jangled so badly that he could hardly remember to reply to her questions politely.

By 2:00, half a dozen prospective buyers had shown up. Travis excused himself, went to the restroom, and then quietly slipped out the patio door. There were a series of connecting trails behind the development that meandered down through the woods, ending at the lake. It felt safe out here in the middle of nowhere; although he didn't delude himself into thinking he was out of danger. Civilization was just a mile over the hill and so were Shaw's men.

The real estate agent locked the office door at dusk, tossed the open house signs in her van, and drove off. Travis went to the back of the model and opened the bathroom window he had unlocked earlier. With a great deal of huffing and puffing, he somehow managed to squeeze his plump frame through the small opening.

The secluded office was a perfect place to stay for the night. He would make good use of the phone, computer, and fully stocked refrigerator. Upstairs he found a small television on the floor in a master suite.

Travis surveyed his bad knee, which was now the color of an overripe eggplant. He applied ice to the joint to reduce the swelling. Afterwards, he took a long relaxing shower. When he was finished, he felt reinvigorated, calmer, and more determined than ever. Most importantly, he could think clearly again. He went downstairs to the refrigerator and pulled out the platter of finger sandwiches, made some coffee, and sat down at the desk.

Removing an address book from his backpack, he turned on the computer and entered the number of Hexxon Communications Systems. Once connected to the server, he typed in his access and security codes. He searched until he found the files he was looking for, which he downloaded on a compact disc. Travis looked at his watch. He had about eighteen hours before anyone would detect what he had done. His confidence had returned, and he smiled.

"One down, one to go." He grabbed a handful of the tuna fish squares off the plate and stuffed them in his mouth as he pulled Marcus's business card from his wallet.

CHAPTER

"Mr. St. John, you have an incoming call from Mr. Travis on your business line," said the security guard.

"Good. Keep him on the line and have someone bring one of the speakerphones over here, fast!" Marcus said. "Looks like we got that luck you said we needed, Doc. Travis is on the line."

When the phone arrived, Sydney hooked it up to a secured line and pushed the speaker button.

"Travis, this is Marcus St. John."

"Mr. St. John, I need your help to get out of here. Shaw's men are crawling all over the place looking for me, and it'll only be a matter of time before they find me."

Doc leaned over to make sure he could be heard. "Mr. Travis, where are you?"

"Who are *you*?" Travis asked suspiciously.

"My name is Julian Sebasst; I'm Mr. St. John's partner. Where are you calling from?"

"Let's just say I'm currently mobile. Tomorrow I'll be somewhere else. Can you get me out of here?"

"Why should I care what happens to you? You're responsible for the death of Anna Mateo," Marcus interjected.

"I didn't know Desmond would have her killed, I swear."

Marcus had had enough. "Shut the hell up. We know this was never about exposing Shaw and his operation. If that was the case, you could have done it years ago. You were blackmailing him and I want to know why. What's so damn valuable that my friend had to die?"

"Nothing other than what I told you. Shaw will do anything to get his hands on the files I have. Believe me, that's all there is."

"I don't have to believe anything. In fact, I don't. I don't remember you ever telling me anything about you being Shaw's cousin and that he might have murdered your parents. What other piece of information have you left out?"

The phone line was quiet. "I could never find anything to link Shaw to my father's death," he whimpered.

"Let me make sure I have this right. You suspected Shaw killed your father, but you went to work for him anyway, because you couldn't prove it. And then, for reasons only you can explain, you choose to expose him. But instead of going to the police, you decide to talk to an obscure reporter. You get her killed and then you want to blab to me—someone you don't know jack shit about, and apparently don't care. Are you starting to see a problem with this picture? It doesn't make sense. And the reason is that you're lying your ass off. Goodbye, Travis."

"Wait! Wait! I'll give you what you want, but you have to promise to help me." Travis sounded more and more desperate.

"I'm not making any deals with you until you tell me what I want to know."

"Okay, look, I've got records of transactions, bribes to public officials and the police, even transcripts of private conversations Shaw had with a couple of high-ranking officials in the Republican Party."

"I've heard this before. Tell me something else!" Marcus shouted.

"Okay, okay! A couple of weeks ago I was trying to reconcile some fund accounts and discovered an irregularity in the books."

"What kind of irregularity?" Marcus asked.

"There was a new payable account under the name of someone named Edmund Lawrence. I checked our records and couldn't find anybody with that name in the company. I snooped around Shaw's office and found the secret set of books he keeps on the *unofficial* people he has working for him. I found the initials E.L. next to an Internet address. I tried accessing the site, but couldn't log on without a password. I figured if Desmond went to all that trouble to camouflage what he was up to, it must be important and worth something. I admit I may have tried to take advantage of the situation, but I only asked for what was rightfully owed to me. He wouldn't even have a company had it not been for the money he swindled from my father."

"What's the web address you tried accessing?" Marcus asked.

"I don't remember. I had it written on a piece paper, but lost it in flight. I…" Travis's mouth went dry.

"Keep talking, Travis."

"I'm really sorry about Anna Mateo. I really am. I knew Shaw would find out I was talking to a reporter and thought he would pay me what he owes me. I never expected him to panic and kill her."

"Just what I thought. You used her, you--."

Doc pulled Marcus by the shirtsleeve and sat him down to cool off. "Travis, tell me what you know about my sister, Eva Ward. What happened to her?"

Travis groaned. "Your sister? I…I don't know exactly what happened that night. Shaw told me to make sure the service door in the basement was unlocked because they needed to get into the building unseen. It wasn't until a few days later that I figured out Shaw must have killed her."

Doc took a calming breath. "Why did he want her dead?"

"It wasn't Shaw; it was Alpine. He was head of the Planning

Commission at the time and your sister worked for the City Planning Department. All I know is they didn't get along and Alpine wanted her gone, and he went to Shaw for help. That's it. I don't know anything more."

"What happened to her body?"

"I don't know."

"Give me a name, Travis. Who killed her?"

"Some freelancer Shaw brought in. I never knew his name."

"What about Leon-Francis? Was he involved in the murders?"

"Hell, yes! He sanctions all hits. They can't do anything without his say-so. He's got people everywhere. He's been grooming Alpine for a long time and it's about to pay off. If he gets elected to the Senate, his next stop is going to be the White House."

"That's impossible," Doc said.

"Nothing's impossible when Leon-Francis is pulling the strings. They've already brokered a deal with the Republican leadership. Next spring, the president is dropping Lauren Dillon, and guess who he's going to select as his new VP? With Leon-Francis behind him, you better believe Alpine is not stopping there. Somehow he'll end up in the oval office."

"Where are you getting all this information, Travis?" Marcus asked.

"That's not important. What *is* important is that I have real, tangible evidence you can use to get these guys. Without it, you won't be able to touch them. Look, we're both in a bind here. You want to nail them and I want to get as far away from them as possible. Neither can happen unless we help each other. You get me out of here and I guarantee I'll give you enough evidence to put all those bastards, including Leon-Francis, in jail for life."

"How do we know you'll keep your word if we help?" Doc asked warily.

"Give me your e-mail address," Travis said.

Marcus motioned to Max to get his laptop.

Three minutes later a blinking red cursor signaled that an e-mail had arrived.

"Did you get it?" Travis asked.

Marcus still wasn't convinced, and he could see that Sydney wasn't either. "Yes, what is it?"

"The information you need to get Shaw."

Max tried unsuccessfully to open the mail. "The file is encrypted. We need the password," he whispered.

"What's the password, Travis?" Marcus demanded.

"First, are you going to help me or not? I've given you what you want."

"Okay, I'll help you. I can be in Evergreen by tomorrow morning."

Doc shook his head. He didn't trust Travis for a second.

"I'm not in Evergreen," the man muttered, "but I can meet you at the airport."

"Give us a number where you can be reached." Marcus managed to keep his tone flat, but inside he was seething.

"That's not going to do you any good. I'm leaving here at dawn and I don't have a cell phone."

"How far are you from Boeing Airfield?" Doc asked.

"About eight or nine miles, I think. Is that where you're landing?"

"Yes, we'll be getting in around 9:30. Meet us there," Doc said.

"I'll be there. So, you'll get me out of the country?"

Closing his eyes as if to keep his anger under control, Marcus said, "If the information is what you say it is, yes."

"Okay. The password to open the file is DLF in caps." The telephone line went dead.

"Travis? Travis! He hung up on us," Marcus shouted. "I think he's nuts."

"Let's see." Max typed in the letters and waited for the file to open.

"Do you believe him?" Marcus asked as they all watched the screen.

"I don't trust anyone who would work for a man who killed his own family," Doc said.

"And I don't believe he forgot that damn website address either--if there even is one."

Rows of numbers suddenly started scrolling down the screen. Max hit the down key and more numbers appeared. "What's with this gibberish?"

"What the--" Marcus sputtered.

"It's in code," Doc said. He reached over Max's shoulder and hit the "end" key." "Two hundred and twenty one pages of code. This is going to take awhile."

●   ●   ●

"I don't want any more excuses. Just get it done!" Shaw slammed the phone down. "Idiots, that's who I've got working for me--incompetent idiots. We've got dozens of people combing the area, and they can't find one witless idiot. On top of that, St. John found the bugs the Colonel's men planted. Security at his house is so tight now a roach couldn't get in."

"How the hell did he find out?" Alpine asked.

"I don't know, but he did. We'll be in deep trouble if we can't get to Travis before St. John does."

Alpine chewed on his lower lip; a nervous habit he hadn't been able to break. "Isn't the Colonel proceeding with the plan tonight?"

"He says his men can get past the security, but I have my doubts. I don't believe a damn thing they tell me anymore. Travis is about as smart as a cricket. If Kilgor and the Colonel can't find him, what makes you think they're capable of getting to St. John?"

Alpine sat motionless in the back seat of the limousine. This was the first time he had seen fear in Shaw's eyes. The man who had always been in control was suddenly running scared. For the first time, Alpine saw his political dream fading. "I think we'd better consider the alternate plan, Desmond."

"You're right. It's time to minimize the damage." Shaw reached for the telephone again.

CHAPTER

A modified police SWAT van sat parked in a vacant lot east of the airport. Kilgor and the Colonel used it as their mobile office and communications center.

The Colonel was on the radio talking with his man in San Francisco. "We've got to get St. John now. You've got one chance and you'd better make it good."

"We're in place and ready to move, sir."

"Good. But if you can't deliver the merchandise successfully, proceed with the alternate plan. Under no circumstances do I want St. John and his friends left alive. Make it look like an accident, but if you have to, shoot them. Do whatever it takes, but make sure they die tonight. Are we clear on this, captain?"

"Affirmative: they're not leaving, sir."

The Colonel removed the headset and turned to face Kilgor, who sat at the other console. "What's the status with Travis?"

"We're still looking. We still have the airport, buses, and cabs covered. We'll get him, don't you worry about that. I'm more concerned about your men, and if they'll get the job done."

"Rangers don't screw up," the Colonel scoffed.

CHAPTER

After lunch, Doc went for a short walk in the woods and used the time to return Asha's telephone call.

"How are you? Are you all right?" she asked.

He was surprised by how glad he was to hear her voice. "I'm fine. I just miss you."

"Me too, love. And I'm worried. I wish you weren't involved."

"Asha, I have to help Marcus. He's in some deep trouble. I can't just walk away."

"I know. If you could, you wouldn't be the man you are. It's just that murder and political intrigue are hard for me to accept. Especially because you're in danger. I know you love Marcus, but I love you, Julian. Promise me you'll take care of yourself, all right?"

"Nothing is going to happen to me, I swear. I still owe you a ride in the plane, remember?"

"Yes, I remember, and I'm holding you to it."

Doc smiled in spite of himself. "Good. How's Carl doing?"

"Fine. He's keeping your dogs at his house until you get back."

"That's a good idea."

"And," Asha added, "Chamberlain wasn't happy about your

sudden departure. Jamal says the campus buzz is that Chamberlain may force you out."

"He's probably ecstatic that I'm gone. I have to admit to a certain relief in knowing that I may not have to work with him. My only regret is the students. They deserved better."

"That couldn't be helped. Anyone in your situation would have made the same decision. Anyway, you still have some support at the university. Your job may still be waiting for you when you get back."

"Don't bet on it. As long as Chamberlain has anything to say about it. Besides, I don't know if I want to go--"

Asha interrupted him. "Excuse me a minute."

Doc heard murmuring in the background, and then she returned to the phone.

"Sorry, that was Jamal. I have a little emergency I need to take care of."

"I'd better let you go."

"No, it'll only take a minute. Jamal wants to talk to you. I'll be back in a jiffy."

Jamal came on the line. "Dr. Sebasst?"

"Hi, Jamal, what's up?"

"I don't have long to talk before Miss Panther gets back. I thought you might want to know that some people are asking around the islands about you."

"What people?"

"One man is called Spoon, or something like that. I don't know the names of the others, but none of them look like the kind of people you would hang around with. They have too many questions."

"Like what?"

"Where you are, when are you coming back, where do you live--things like that."

Doc tensed. He didn't like the sound of this. "How many?"

"I've only seen three, but I think there could be at least one more, because their cell phones never stop ringing."

"Tell me more about Spoon. What does he look like?"

"He's white, about my size, but a lot older. He has brown hair and a big bald spot on the top of his head, and speaks with a southern accent."

Doc didn't know anybody who fit that description. "Can you try and get more information?"

"Yes, sir."

"I'm going to give you my cell phone number and I want you to call me whenever you have something. Anytime of the day or night; it doesn't matter, understand?"

"Oh, yes. I understand very well."

But Doc wasn't satisfied. "And Jamal?"

"Yes?"

"Keep a close eye on Ms. Panther for me."

"I always do, Dr. Sebasst."

CHAPTER

Two black Dodge vans pulled off the dirt road near Pondsmith Road. The air was crisp for a September night, with a slight howl of wind echoing through the black forest. The captain stepped from the vehicle and joined the men clustered in a semi-circle, awaiting orders.

"Gentlemen, I don't need to remind you that we're being paid very handsomely for our services by our employer. He expects, and will settle for, nothing less than success on our mission. Nor will I. Our target is three and a half clicks southwest through the woods. St. John likes his privacy. His estate sits in the middle of a forty-eight acre wilderness preserve he has in trust. The only vulnerable spot, and way to breach the property undetected is from the north by the guesthouse. Sarge is already in position and will rendezvous with you at 0100 at these coordinates." The captain pointed to the map. "Once you arrive at your positions, you know the drill. The objective is stealth, gentlemen. We don't want them to see us coming. The perimeter is surrounded by civilians. The heat pump is located on the north side of the main house. Disconnect the compressor, attach the containers, and leave. You should be back here by 0230. If for any reason you are spotted, terminate any witnesses. Is that clear?"

"Yes, sir," they said in unison.

"Good. I'll see you back here at 0230."

The soldiers collected their weapons and gear from the van, three of them strapping silver canisters to their backs. They attached night-vision headgear and headed south.

Cartwright, leader of the little platoon and designated point man, led the men through the black forest until they reached a small lake, which they had to detour around. The closer they got to the estate, the more the trail narrowed. The trek through the forest ended an hour later when they reached a giant briar patch that stood as high as a basketball rim. Sarge and his men were waiting for them.

Sarge adjusted his headset and called the captain. "The fox is in the hen house and we're ready to rock-n-roll," he whispered.

"Good. Maintain radio silence until you've achieved the objective."

"Yes, sir." Sarge handed the radio to one of his men and turned to Cartwright. "The fence is on the other side of the briars. We'll wait at the gates just in case something goes wrong. The men separated into three teams—each caring a silver canister. Sarge's team circled around toward the south gate, while a second team veered right toward the back gate and pool. Cartwright's men forged straight ahead through the briar patch.

Even with night vision, it was difficult for Cartwright to see where they were going. Thickets of razor thorns easily penetrated their camouflage uniforms as they crept closer. They could see the house now, about one hundred and sixty yards away. No guards near the fence. He saw something else, too. Just to the right was a narrow trail running parallel along the fence. It ended in front of some bushes that seemed out of place. Cartwright moved in for a closer look and then recognized his mistake.

"Shit!" he screamed as a burst of white light hit them all in the eyes.

●　●　●

Doc was on the terrace smoking a cigar when he heard the deafening explosion, and saw a man catapulted onto the fence. Flames shot from the woods followed by screams and automatic gunfire. He grabbed a gun from Marcus's desk and jumped over the terrace rail down to the patio. He was first to reach the dead soldier straddling the wrought iron fence. Doc pushed the body off, climbed over the fence, and ran thirty yards to the edge of the briars. The sky above was engulfed in light. There was more shooting, screams—and then silence. At that moment the lights went out.

Marcus came running across the lawn wearing only his briefs, with his men close behind. When they got to the fence, Marcus saw Doc trying to find an entrance through the briar field. "Doc, what the hell is going on over there?"

"I don't know, but it's coming from somewhere in there."

"That's impossible! No animal, much less a man, could be in there," Marcus said.

"Well, I know what I heard. How can I get through this?"

"Didn't you hear me? It's too thick to penetrate!"

"Then get me something I can use to cut through it!"

Marcus told his guards to run to the house and get what his partner needed.

The men brought back a floodlight and machete, passing them to Doc through the fencing. Gunfire erupted again, but this time it came from the back gate. Marcus saw Sydney in the distance, running towards the woods with two of the guards.

"You men stay here with Doc," Marcus shouted as he took off running toward the house.

● ● ●

When Sarge heard the explosion and gunfire on the north end of the estate, he knew Cartwright had failed. It was time to go with option

B. He radioed the other team at the south gate to move in. A bullet whizzed by his head—and then another.

"What's happening?" Sarge shrieked as he tried to find cover. The soldier carrying the silver canister got hit. A second bullet punctured the canister, exploding Freon in the soldier's face. He screamed, clutching his frozen eyes with his hands, and died. Three more soldiers yelled as bullets tore through flesh. Sarge heard a loud roar—just before his head flew off and rolled up against the gate.

*   *   *

Marcus saw men moving cautiously toward the back of the house. He cut through the tennis court to the back side of the garden, taking two steps at a time up to the house. Just beyond the back gate, he saw flashlights moving in the woods. Sydney and her men.

He turned when he heard the sound of breaking twigs behind him. Four black-clad figures with automatic weapons moved swiftly across the lawn. He eased back under the shadows of the eaves. When the men reached the step landing, they spread out. Marcus swore under his breath when he realized he didn't have a weapon. Two of the men moved quickly toward the main house, while the other two maintained sentry positions by the gazebo and swimming pool.

Marcus was seventeen feet behind the gazebo. He crawled between the shrubs, circling as he went until he reached the back steps. He crawled across the cedar floor, pausing when he was a few feet from the masked soldier. Marcus eased up behind him, twisted his neck, and gently lowered the dead soldier to the ground.

The silent kill didn't go unnoticed. Marcus felt the air move as a bullet passed his head. He snatched the soldier's rifle off the ground and ran. Bullets chased him as he dove across the cabana bar.

The shooter rushed him, spraying the stainless steel bar with bullets until the rifle was empty. He fumbled, trying to get the extra clip from his pocket, but dropped it when Marcus popped up from behind the bar with a rifle in his hands. Marcus squeezed the trigger, but the gun jammed. Marcus charged the man and tackled him before he had a chance to pick the clip off the ground.

The soldier pulled his revolver, but Marcus knocked it out of his hand. They grappled on the grass, fighting for control of the gun. When the soldier tried to kick him with the heel of his boot, Marcus locked onto his leg and dragged him away. That's when he felt the knife sheath strapped to the man's ankle. He ripped the knife free, turned the stranger over, and plunged the blade into his heart.

Marcus rolled over to catch his breath and saw two more men running toward him. They open-fired and a dozen bullets bounced off the concrete, inches from his feet. He fell back into the swimming pool, ducking under water in a desperate attempt to evade the men, but there was no place for him to hide. He came up for air just in time to hear gunshots and see both soldiers drop into the pool. Sydney holstered her gun and ran to make sure Marcus was unharmed.

* * *

Doc worked his way through thirty feet of thick bramble before reaching the dead soldiers. They looked like alien bug-eyed monsters with their bulging night scopes fused to their faces, and their bodies impaled on thorns, riddled with bullets. He noticed the odd-shaped silver canister on the ground next to a dead soldier. When he reached out to touch it, sensor-activated halogen lights flashed on and he saw two camouflaged smoking turret machine guns.

"Doc! Doc! Are you in there?" Marcus yelled as he climbed into a truck with Sydney behind the wheel.

"Yes," he shouted back.

"Get out of here, fast. We've got a line on these guys. We're going after them. Hurry!"

Sydney started the truck and honked the horn. "Come on Doc, we gotta go, gotta go!"

Marcus opened the door as the truck pulled out of the gate.

Doc emerged from the briars at that moment, jumped in and slammed the door as the truck screeched down the road.

"One of our people saw a suspicious van parked a few miles up the road," Sydney explained breathlessly. "We're going to check it out." She paused. "What did you find out there?"

"You don't want to know," Doc said.

"Yeah, I figured as much. We found a few mutilated corpses ourselves behind the guesthouse," Marcus said.

Glancing at his friend, Doc raised his eyebrows. "You decide to take a late night swim?"

Marcus looked at his soaked body and bare legs, and realized how ridiculous he must look. "It's a long story."

"Yeah, I bet. Were any of your people hurt?"

"Two in the house are down. No one saw anything until after the smoke, and by then it was over. A headless wonder and four dead men by the pool were packing army tags," Sydney said. She made a sudden sharp left turn off the narrow road onto an even narrower road dotted with deep ruts and potholes. She thrust the clutch into first and accelerated. The truck heaved and sank as they flew down the rough road.

Marcus and Doc shouted her name as she shifted into third.

"What? You want to catch these guys, don't you? This is a shortcut to Rockingport Road."

"Yeah, we want to get there, too--but alive," Marcus said.

Doc spotted the black vans off the side of the road. "There! Over there!" he pointed.

Sydney slammed her foot on the brakes, and the truck skidded off the road, barely missing a tree as it came to a stop.

One van still had its headlights on. Doc and Sydney cautiously approached with guns drawn. Inside were the captain and two of his men with bullets in their heads.

Marcus pounded his fist on the van in frustration.

Sydney tucked her gun into her waistband. "I don't understand this. If these are the guys that were after us, who killed them?"

Doc knelt in the dirt, inspecting a set of tire tracks. "Jumbies," he said.

Marcus looked blank. "Jumbies? What's that?"

"Caribbean folklore. They're the kings of the underworld—the bogeymen. And it looks like they went that way," Doc said, pointing to the woods.

CHAPTER

30

The Police Department has issued an All Points Bulletin for Dana Travis, purportedly responsible for robbing the Venture Capital Bank two days ago. Travis is considered armed and dangerous. Anyone having information concerning his whereabouts is asked to call the Evergreen Police Department.

Travis rested on the king-sized bed, still trying to wrap his mind around the news he had just heard for the second time. Desmond Shaw was crafty--always had been, but even Travis was surprised that he was resorting to this. His picture would be plastered across the front page of every local newspaper by morning. Now, instead of worrying about Shaw's thugs, he was going to have to evade the police of three different jurisdictions as well. The noose was tightening around his neck.

He shuddered and sat up in bed, reflecting on the cold reality of his situation. Who was he fooling; did he really expect to outsmart Shaw? This wasn't "The Fugitive" and he wasn't Richard Kimble. This was the real world and in the real world Travis didn't have any friends to help him. No one but Marcus St. John.

Getting to Boeing Airfield would be damn near impossible; the police would be there looking for him. His head throbbed and he started feeling sorry for himself. That was something he'd done a lot of over the years. He decided to do something he'd never tried before. He dropped to his knees to pray, but not to ask forgiveness or repent. He was an unregenerate man, who wasn't sorry for anything he had done. Instead, the prayer he offered to his God was simple and profane.

"I've never asked you for anything in this life, so I figure you owe me at least one request. You know I need a miracle to pull this off. If you will just help me out this one time, I swear I won't ask you for anything else."

Travis didn't feel the sense of peace that others professed to experience when they've communicated with God, and he had no assurance the prayer had been heard.

Dejected and exhausted, he resettled himself in bed and turned off the television. In a few hours he would leave for the airport, and he had no idea how he was going to get there. Of equal concern was the kind of response he would get from St. John, once St. John realized he had been deceived.

❋   ❋   ❋

The Colonel sat in the van, trying to decide what to do next. He hadn't heard from his men in two hours, even though he was supposed to receive hourly updates.

Something was wrong, Kilgor could feel it. "Try to reach him again on the radio."

"I can't risk it. The police may have the van and could be monitoring incoming calls. We'll just have to wait until he contacts us."

"Contacts us! The mission should have been completed an hour ago and your team should have called us by now." Kilgor's eyes narrowed. "If they were planning on calling in the first place."

"What do you mean by that?" It wasn't the first time the man had cast aspersions on he and his men, and the Colonel had had enough of it.

"Just what I said. The captain and your good ole' boys may have decided to take our money and run. Maybe this was a setup and you never intended to whack St. John. I told Shaw from the get-go not to trust you burned out, over-the-hill GI Joes. We should have taken care of this ourselves."

Faster than a leopard attacking its prey, the Colonel sprang from his chair, delivering a crushing blow to the side of the bigger man's head. Kilgor crashed to the floor. When he opened his eyes, the Colonel was sitting on his chest with a .45 jammed down his throat.

"I'm tired of you, Kilgor. Have been for some time. People like you and Shaw don't have a spine. If you did, you never would have hired us to do your dirty work in the first place. I have a mind to end your miserable existence right now," he hissed, leaning toward Kilgor's face. "But I've got more pressing issues to deal with, like finding out what happened to my men. I don't care what you and Shaw think of me, but I take personal offense to your disparaging remarks about my men and their integrity. So keep your damn mouth shut. Do we have an understanding?"

Kilgor's eyes blazed with anger. He wanted to rip the Colonel apart with his bare hands.

"Do we have an understanding?" the Colonel repeated while keeping the gun firmly in place.

Kilgor blinked in agreement.

The Colonel holstered his pistol, climbed off the big man, and calmly reoccupied his chair as though nothing had happened. "You'd better save what energy you have for Desmond. He's going to want to know what happened and I don't have any answers right now."

"No shit, Sherlock," Kilgor spat. If your people were caught, they might talk. And if they do, I want to be on the first train smokin' from here."

The Colonel looked at him in disgust. "My men don't know enough about our operations. Anyway, they won't talk; they're professionals."

"Yeah, right, just like you told me they wouldn't screw up."

*   *   *

Shaw's instincts told him St. John was still alive. He crushed an empty beer can and threw it at the wastebasket in disgust. It missed.

The name of the game now was to eliminate either Travis or St. John. Simple really. St. John couldn't do anything without Travis and he couldn't get anywhere without St. John's help. If St. John were still stupid enough to come to Evergreen, it would make his job even easier. Shaw turned off the lights and tried to relax, but the telephone interrupted him again. It was Kilgor.

"We think we found Travis. Some real estate lady called the station fifteen minutes ago. She recognized his picture on the tube and swears it's the same man she met this morning in Duwamish. I've got some guys on the way to check it out."

"Good. Let me know what you find. I'm on my way home, so call me on my cell when you know something. Any news from San Francisco yet?"

"Negative. It's my guess they botched the job. I've got some local police friends down there checking it out. I'll call you when I hear something."

Suddenly, Shaw's cell phone rang. "I've got another call coming in. I'll get back to you." *Who is calling me on my private line this time of the night?* he wondered.

"Mr. Shaw, this is Jason Worrick. I wanted to let you know that someone broke into our computer system tonight and downloaded some files from our classified archives. We're still trying to ascertain which files were tampered with. Some of our associates will be arriving in Evergreen in the morning."

Shaw felt sick. "Why?"

"We traced the hacker to your area. Mr. Leon-Francis is concerned that whatever was stolen may be prejudicial to his interests, and that's why he's sending an investigative team. He wants you at the airport when they arrive and he expects your full cooperation in this matter. The flight arrives at 10:40, United Airlines, flight 216. Be there."

"I've got a press conference at 11:30 there's no way I ca--"

Worrick hung up.

Shaw sank back in his chair, stunned and more than a little queasy. His world was unraveling faster than a spool of yarn rolling down hill, and he couldn't stop it. Getting a call from Jason Worrick was like getting one from the police—it got your immediate attention and it usually wasn't good. Worrick was Leon-Francis's personal secretary. The inflection and tone of his voice could foretell one's future. Judging by the brief call, Shaw knew he was in trouble. What he didn't know was why anyone would want to hack the Excalibur Group's files.

Then it hit him like a sledgehammer to his chest. He frantically patted his pocket to make sure his key was still there, and it was. He relaxed—until another thought hit him.

He jumped to his feet and grabbed the phone. "Kilgor, it's me again. Tell your men I want Travis taken alive. Do you hear me?"

"I thought you wanted him shot on sight?"

"The information he's carrying may be on a computer disk or memory stick, so I want him alive until we know for sure. I'm going to spend the rest of the night at the office, so contact me here when you have some news."

He took a hot shower in his office bathroom before lying down on the couch. In the morning he'd call Alpine to let him know he couldn't make the press conference. He had no idea what he would say to Leon-Francis's men when they arrived, but he'd think of something; he always did.

Still, his fingers trembled, just a little, and he locked them together, revolted by his own weakness.

What really bothered him was Dana Travis. He was proving to be a lot smarter—and more dangerous--than Shaw had thought.

CHAPTER

J amal Calderon made it a point to go into the restaurant lounge Every fifteen minutes to check on the two men loitering at the bar. For the last two days they'd become regular customers of The French Quarter. Their lunch had become as predictable as the cheap linen suites they wore every day. They ordered lobster, dolphin, and black beer while they waited for Spoon to arrive. He usually arrived late.

Jamal's cousin was the night attendant at the hotel where the men stayed. They were frequent visitors of the man sequestered in Room 23, known as M. Beale. Beale seldom left his room except to go downstairs to the hotel bar. All his meals were delivered to his room, and he refused maid service.

Monitoring the men's activities for Dr. Sebasst wasn't easy, and finding out what they were up to was even harder.

While Beale was obviously keeping a low profile, Spoon and his men spent their time scurrying around the islands searching for something. For what? Jamal didn't know, but it couldn't be good.

In two days, the men had spent time at The Division of Records and Archives in St. Thomas, the public library on St. John Island, and had taken a boat trip to Tortola Island, which was off the northern coast of St. John. But what worried Jamal the most was Spoon.

Earlier this morning, Jamal had followed him as far as East St. Croix, where Spoon rented a SUV and drove to Fredericksted. The sparsely populated area was tucked away in the northwestern corner of the Island where Dr. Sebasst lived.

After Spoon's men gobbled up their lunch, they waited around for him, but he never showed up. Jamal wondered where he was.

❋ ❋ ❋

Spoon's assignment was proving to be more arduous than his cohorts. It took some effort for him to find a way over the seven foot wall that surrounded the isolated villa burrowed into the hillside that overlooked the ocean. He followed a narrow path, which ran along the edge of the cliff and ended up at the back of the bronzed-colored stucco estate.

The three-storied villa with a roof pavilion was hidden by coconut palms and Bougainvillea plants. Spoon crept closer until he had a clear view. He saw an outdoor swimming pool extending past large glass doors into the villa.

Twenty minutes later the doors slid back into walls and Asha swam out as she did every afternoon for her daily swim.

CHAPTER

Travis heard the car coming before it turned the corner. He jumped up, fully dressed. He had learned from experience to sleep in his clothes with one eye open. From the window he saw the car circle the cul-de-sac and stop in front of the office. Three men got out. He recognized the man in front, wearing a black trench coat. His name was Carter and he was the head of Shaw Security.

"Fan out. You men check out the units on this block and work your way back around the cul-de-sac. I'll check out the office and the houses on this side and pick you up around the corner," Carter said.

Travis grabbed his backpack, ran downstairs and out the sliding glass door. The large Douglas Firs obliterated the moonlight, making it difficult for him to see where he was going. He stumbled into a trashcan full of metal roofing scraps. The noise reverberated through the woods.

"There! Over there! I see him," shouted one of the men. Travis sprang to his feet and darted down the narrow trail leading to the lake. He was too heavy and out of shape to outrun his pursuers, but he had an advantage. He knew where he was going.

The trail forked at the entrance and looped around the lake. There was only one way in and one way out, but they didn't know that. With some difficulty, he removed the sign that read "3.5 Mile Loop" and tossed it in the weeds. Then he hobbled ninety feet down the trail and took cover behind a fallen tree.

The men stopped when they reached the trail entrance. One of them pulled out a map and a flashlight.

"You! Call the boys and tell them to get over here. I want this whole area sealed. The woods extend to Harris Road, so get some men over there in case he comes out the back end."

Three more men arrived while he was talking.

"You three take that trail. You two—come with me."

Travis heard noise, but couldn't see much. They had split their forces as he anticipated, but he knew reinforcements would soon be on their way. In a few minutes the place would be crawling with security guards. If he was going to make his escape, he had to do it now.

He reached into his backpack and slowly removed a gun. The sound of footsteps grew closer as the men inched their way along the trail. Travis realized he had chosen a poor location to make a stand. The lake was directly to his back, offering no place for retreat if he needed it. He slid onto his back under a fallen tree, hidden by rotted limbs with his face pressed against the sappy bark.

One of the men stepped on top of the tree stump to get a better look. When he turned around, he found himself staring down the barrel of a Magnum. Travis shot him in the chest and then turned and shot a second man, who stumbled backward, clutching his stomach. The third guard panicked and shot blindly into the dark.

The guards on the other trail doubled back when they heard the gunfire. When they arrived, they found three dead men on the ground. Carter motioned for them to circle around, but the Magnum erupted again, hurling one man against a stump.

Carter jumped behind a tree and fired. "To hell with taking this guy alive."

Minutes later, three more black Suburbans arrived, loaded with men wearing the black and yellow leather jackets bearing the Shaw Security logo.

The Swat van carrying Kilgor and the Colonel arrived at the subdivision twenty minutes later. Kilgor had a difficult time maneuvering the large van around the parked Suburbans. He tried parking in the cul-de-sac, only to find himself staring into the head beams of one of the black monoliths with the ominous black-tinted windows.

"Damn, why don't Shaw's men drive normal vehicles like the rest of the world, instead of those monster trucks that take up the whole damn road?" Kilgor slammed the van into reverse and backed up onto the sidewalk so the truck could get through. The driver waved to him through the partially open window as he passed.

"Bastard!" Kilgor snarled.

The development was lit up like a Christmas tree from all the floodlights. Carter had transformed the office into a war room. He was sitting at the desk, barking orders on the phone, when Kilgor entered. "I don't care what you have to do, get that helicopter up in the air and search the area again!" He banged the phone down on the desk. "We must have close to thirty men searching the woods and we still can't find him."

"You sure he didn't get past you?" Kilgor asked.

"I don't know how he could. We've got this whole area sealed up tighter than a Ziploc bag. The only way he's getting out of here is if he's invisible or dead."

"I told you, take him alive. He's got some information we need."

"Alive! That little bastard killed some of my people."

"I don't care if he killed your wife; we need him alive. Get on the horn to your guys and pass the word—no shooting."

The Colonel's phone vibrated. He checked the message. "Your friends from San Francisco are calling."

Kilgor stepped outside and took the call. A moment later he was back in the office. "Your men didn't make it. The police found them in the woods near St. John's place—dead. Your captain was in the van with a bullet hole the size of an acorn in his head."

"Who did it?"

"Don't know. St. John's attorney swears it wasn't them."

"That's crap!" the Colonel snapped. "Who else could it have been?"

"Whoever it was, they knew we were coming and were ready."

"This is worse than bad," the Colonel said.

"The whole thing stinks," Kilgor agreed. "Our people were the only ones who knew about this. Somebody talked and I'm going to find out who."

The discussion was interrupted by noise coming from the street.

One of the guards looked out the window. "They got him!"

Kilgor ran out in time to see four men carrying a limp body soaked in blood. He pushed his way through the crowd to get to it.

"He's dead," said one of the men.

Kilgor cursed and shoved everyone out of his way. "I told you I wanted him alive!"

The body lay face down in the grass. The back of his skull was crushed. Kilgor knelt and turned the man over.

"It's Griffin. He's one of ours," Carter said angrily.

The Colonel shook his head. "It looks like he ran into Travis."

"Where did you find him?" Kilgor demanded.

"Over there, across the street," a guard said, pointing to a clearing in the woods.

"Spread out; he's out of the woods. Search every inch of this place, all the houses—everything. He can't have gotten far," Kilgor instructed them.

Stunned by the sight of their colleague's body, the men didn't budge. "Move! *Now!*"

The Colonel caught Kilgor by the elbow to get his attention. "I think Travis is already gone."

"What?"

"Remember that Suburban we passed when we came in?"

"Carter!" Kilgor shouted.

Carter stopped.

"We passed one of your men coming in. Where was he going?"

"They're all still here."

"Then who was that we saw leaving in a Suburban?" the Colonel asked.

"All of our trucks are where we left them. I don't know what you're talking about."

"How many vehicles did you bring?" the Colonel asked.

"Five."

"Well, from where I stand I only see four. Looks to me like you lost one."

CHAPTER

The Gulfstream V had just crossed over the Cascades when Marcus returned from the cockpit.

"Quik, you've got enough Intel and communication gear on this plane to start your own revolution," Doc said, sitting at the small computer workstation containing three computers, fax, and satellite communication equipment.

"Never know when it might come in handy. How's the decoding coming?"

"I'm getting there. One thing you can't say about Travis is that he's stupid. He's using a code containing 500 or more numbers. You have to know the right series and sequence in order to decipher it. Finding the right combination and progression takes time."

He typed in another command and four letters scrolled down the screen. "So far I have eighteen letters. I'll have the rest in a few more minutes."

Instead of being excited about cracking Travis's code, Marcus seemed disinterested. He sat on the leather sofa with legs crossed, an unlit cigar in his mouth, staring at the blank television screen in the wall. Doc pushed his swivel rocker away from the counsel. "What's on your mind?"

"I can't believe these lowlifes. They want my ass so bad they don't care about taking out my family too. If they'd been successful in connecting that Freon to my heat pump system, and if Caitlin and the kids had been home, we would all be dead." Just the thought of Caitlin and the girls dying made his blood run cold. I swear I'm going to get them and I don't care what it costs me."

"It may cost plenty," Doc warned.

"What do you *really* think happened to the soldiers in the woods?"

Doc scratched the stubble on his chin. "I'm not sure. I've never seen anything like it in my life. Those men weren't just killed; they were butchered. Those machine guns discharged 1,500 rounds each—enough lead to sink a jumbo ferry."

"But you're thinking Leon-Francis is behind this?"

"From the things you've told me about him, I don't know who else could have pulled it off. Those robotic sentry guns are military issue. The only place I've seen any like them is in the Middle East. They're used for border patrol—protecting isolated and unmanned borders between adversarial countries, like Syria and Iraq or India and Pakistan. Then there's the matter of the claymore mines the police also found. The fact that they could do that on your property without you noticing is even more amazing."

He stared past Marcus. "On the other hand, it doesn't make sense. Why would Leon-Francis kill his own men? *If* they were even working for him. Maybe he just doesn't want you dead--at least not yet."

"Thanks, that's real comforting."

Doc smiled grimly as he turned back to the workstation. The computer screen was filled with letters. "It's finished."

Marcus jumped up from his seat.

Doc typed in some commands and a three-dimensional matrix overlay appeared on the screen. The letters slowly metamorphosed into words.

Marcus stood staring at the jumbled words.

Sydney came rushing through the galley from the cockpit, "You need to turn on the television. Channel 11."

Grasping the remote, Marcus did as she asked. The news was re-broadcasting the story on Dana Travis. "Damn! Doc, look at this!"

Doc was riveted to the computer screen, but he turned around to watch.

"No wonder Travis wants my help," Marcus said.

"Don't you think it's odd that a man fighting to stay alive would take time out to rob a bank?" Sydney asked.

Doc frowned. "Could be Shaw had him set him up."

"Makes sense," Sydney agreed. "With the police after him, he won't get far."

"How are we going to get him out now?" Marcus flopped back into his seat, disgusted.

Doc shrugged, acknowledging that he didn't have the answer.

"I should tell Peri to turn the jet around and head back home. Travis didn't say anything about a shitload of police being on his ass. Since the beginning, he's been lying and manipulating me to his advantage. As far as I'm concerned, Desmond Shaw can use him for target practice."

"I think you're going to want to change your mind after you look at this," Doc said, handing Marcus a printout.

Marcus gave up after a few paragraphs. "It doesn't make sense," he said, tossing the paper back to Doc."

"That's because it's incomplete."

"What—you got a glitch in your program or something?"

"I wish it were that simple. The fact is there's nothing wrong with the decoding. Travis conveniently omitted some key pieces of information. My guess is there's another file somewhere that we need in order to figure this out. He wants to make sure you keep your word."

Marcus's jaw tightened and his eyes were as cold as granite. Travis had played him for a fool again.

A soft woman's voice spoke his name over the intercom.

"Yeah Peri, what's up?"

"Just letting you know we're landing. We should be on the ground in about fifteen minutes. Should I begin our descent?"

Marcus looked at Doc.

"I don't like the odds either, but I dislike the idea of running even more. It only gives Shaw and Alpine another chance to get us at home. I say we keep going. With some luck, Travis will be waiting at the airport, and we can just pick him up and fly out."

"And if he isn't?" Marcus asked.

"Then we're in trouble. We need him or the missing file. I really don't think we have any other options at this point, but it's your call. You're the one with the most to lose. If you want to pack it in and try something else, I'll understand."

Marcus paced the galley, deep in thought. When he stopped, he picked up a marble ashtray off the workstation and flung it at the computer monitor. The screen exploded, shorting out the workstation.

Doc pushed away from the consol." I can see you're not going to be the best person to negotiate with Travis."

* * *

The Colonel was on his second cup of coffee when Desmond Shaw walked into the Top Flight Café, which was next to Sea-Tac Airport. As usual, Shaw was impeccably dressed in a black three-piece suit and his signature duster.

"You look like hell, Colonel," he said as he signaled the waitress for coffee.

"You would too, if you'd been up all night."

"Where's Kilgor?"

"Next door getting some smokes. He'll be back in a minute."

Shaw was about to lay his coat on the barstool when Kilgor came in. "Come on; let's sit in the back so we can have some privacy."

They moved to the small banquet room and shut the door. "Where's Travis?" Shaw asked.

"He could be halfway to Florida now that he has his hands on one of our trucks. We've got every available man looking for the Suburban, but so far nothing," Kilgor said.

Shaw sat, legs crossed, eyeing the two men. "Well, I've talked to my people in California. No one has seen or heard from St. John since early this morning. He and his friends are missing and so is his plane. You can bet your ass he's on his way here to meet Travis. When we find them, we'll find *him*. Make sure our men are covering the airports."

"Over half our people are at Sea-Tac now. How do you expect us to stake them all out?" Kilgor asked.

"You don't have to. There are only a few large enough to accommodate St. John's G5. He's either flying into Sea-Tac, Boeing Field, or Paine Field. I want you two in the van, ready to go, when we get confirmation of the landing. Tell your men not to move until we have both St. John and Travis. Follow them, do whatever you have to, but wait until they make contact before taking them out. I've got some unexpected out-of-town guests coming in this morning and I want these guys out of the way by the time they arrive."

"What if the police get there first?" Kilgor asked.

"What if they do? I pay you good money to take care of the police. I don't care how you do it. Any other questions?"

The Colonel had been quiet until then, but suddenly his face was flushed and his breathing labored. "Yeah, I got one. I want to know who killed my men."

"How would I know?"

"There were only three people aware of our plans, unless you told Alpine, which would make four. Someone realized they were out there and was waiting for them, which means one of us talked."

Shaw rose to his feet, his eyes burning.

For a minute Kilgor thought Shaw was going to hit the Colonel.

"Listen to me. I'm sorry your men are dead, but they got sloppy and that's why they died. I don't like it any more than you, especially since we paid you $2 million to take care of our problems. If you had one ounce of brains in that pea head of yours, you'd know that St. John killed them. He's the only one who could have. I don't care what he told the police. Do you actually think anyone could have gotten onto his property and booby-trapped it without him knowing it? His house and grounds were fortified better than a marine compound."

Shaw moved closer to the Colonel. "Don't you ever get in my face and accuse me of some silly shit like this again. I've got more important things on my mind right now than dealing with your crap." Shaw slung his duster over his shoulder, finished his coffee, and tossed the empty cup on the table. "I want you guys out there, and I want you to stay there until you bring me Travis's head!" He turned and stormed out.

"He's lying through his teeth," the Colonel said.

Kilgor thought so too, but he didn't want to give the Colonel the satisfaction of knowing he was probably right. "Let's hit the streets."

CHAPTER

B oeing Field was the regional airport and cargo hub for Federal Express, DHL, and UPS. With the airport undergoing major renovation, Travis found it easy to slip the Suburban into the parking area ,and park unnoticed alongside the cargo and constructions trucks. He turned the engine off and waited. Some of Shaw's guards passed by, but didn't see him behind the heavily tinted windows. Seven minutes later, he saw a black and silver jet circling to make its approach. Travis put on his sunglasses and got out of the truck. He zipped his security jacket closed to hide the gun tucked into his waistband, and joined the group of guards going through the main door. Airport security directed them to the upstairs mezzanine, which was under construction. A short, attractive brunette met them there.

"Gentlemen, if you would please..." She swept her arm toward a conference room.

"Please, have a seat," she said with a warm smile, once everyone was inside.

Travis sat in a chair at the back of the room.

"My name is Alexia Davidovich and I am Chief of Security

Operations for this airport. You men are being temporarily restricted from the mezzanine during our lockout period."

"Lockout?" someone asked.

Travis realized it was Carter and tried to make himself invisible.

"This is standard security procedure when we have U.S. government personnel arriving. Only airport and government personnel with the appropriate security clearance are authorized to be on this floor."

Carter crossed his arms belligerently. "We're with Shaw Security and are assisting the police in apprehending a wanted criminal we suspect may be trying to use this airport to make his escape."

Alexia smiled at him. "Who are you, again?"

"James Carter."

"Ah, yes. Mr. Carter," she said with a slight Czech accent. "I am fully aware of who you are and your purpose. However, that has no bearing here. This airport is under my jurisdiction and regulations are very clear on this matter. Only personnel authorized by me are permitted to be in the area."

"Well, give us authorization. What's the problem?"

"The problem, Mr. Carter, is that I do not need your help to do my job. Frankly, it astounds me that the Evergreen Police Department would resort to using a private security company to do *their* job, but that's not my concern. What *is* my concern is this airport and maintaining its high level of security integrity. To do that I must insist that you go back downstairs to the lower level, or the waiting room where you and your men may help yourselves to refreshments. The North Terminal will be closed for approximately twenty or thirty minutes. We will notify you when you may re-enter the mezzanine area."

But Carter wasn't willing to let it go. "Who's coming in on the plane?"

"That's classified information on a need-to-know basis only."

"Bitch," he whispered loud enough for everyone to hear.

Alexia ignored him and continued smiling.

The men rose and left the room. She closed the door and was starting to leave, when she observed the funny looking man with sunglasses standing against the wall. "Sir, please follow your friends downstairs."

Travis approached her cautiously. He had already decided that he was going to have to trust her if he stood any chance of getting to Marcus. "I need to see the men coming in on that plane," he said.

"Alexia pulled a revolver from the holster in the small of her back, pointing it at the floor. "I don't know who you are, but you will not be going anywhere near that plane."

"My name is Dana Travis." He removed his cap and sunglasses. "I'm the reason St. John and his partner, Sebasst, is here. They're coming to pick me up. It's imperative that I see him as soon as possible." He took a step forward.

"Stop! I want you to take three steps back, put your hands on your head and turn around."

"Look, I know this looks bad, but I'm no criminal. If the police or those security goons in there get their hands on me, I'm dead. I can't let you arrest me."

"I won't arrest you, but neither will I let you anywhere near that plane."

He had misjudged this woman. She was going to hand him over to the police, and he couldn't allow that to happen. He was too close now to let anyone stand in his way. He slid his right hand slowly into his jacket.

"This is your last warning. Put your hands out where I can see them!"

Travis was running out of time. His fingers tightened on the pistol, until realizing that he had to trust her. There was no way out of this mess unless she helped him. He pulled his hands from the pockets and raised them.

"Okay, but you gotta help me. They're expecting me."

Alexia looked thoughtful, and then slowly lowered her weapon. "Follow me."

Travis breathed a sigh of relief.

She took him to her office and ushered him inside. "I can't break protocol by allowing you in the terminal, even if what you're telling me is true. This floor is a restricted area from everyone except my people. You'll be safe here, just lock the door. I'll bring Julian Sebasst to you."

Travis nodded, but he knew that wouldn't work. The sooner he could get to the plane the faster he could get out of here.

Hurrying now, she raced out of the building and across the tarmac to a waiting jeep. "Has the airplane landed?" she asked as she jumped into the front seat.

"Yes, ma'am, everything is in place and they're waiting for you to board," said the driver.

"Let's get out there." The jeep turned in a semi-circle and sped off to the north terminal.

●　　●　　●

Carter had decided that he and his men would wait outside in the parking lot. As soon as he saw Alexia leaving the building, he stomped out his cigarette and ordered his men back into the airport. Halfway up the stairs to the mezzanine, he saw a man wearing a Shaw Security jacket duck into one of the offices in the long hallway.

Something was wrong. He did another head count but all his men were present. He called Kilgor. "We've got a problem out here. Some VIP is landing, and the woman in charge won't let us near the airstrip."

"Have you seen the plane?" Kilgor asked.

"No, they pulled us off before it landed. Another thing, do you have more of our men out here that I don't know about?"

"No, I don't. Get your men going and find out who it is, and who is on that airplane! We're on our way," Kilgor shouted.

Carter ran to Alexia's office. The door was locked. He kicked it open—and saw the side door swinging on its hinges. On the other side was the mezzanine.

* * *

The cabin door opened and Doc stepped out. "Alexia good to see you."

"It's been a long time, Julian."

They exchanged awkward kisses and he introduced her to Marcus and Sydney.

"Thanks for the last minute security. There are some men that might not want us here."

She nodded. "That's what I've been hearing. A man named Dana Travis is anxious to see you."

"So he made it. Where is he?" Marcus asked.

"Waiting in my office, but I'm afraid he's in a lot of trouble."

"Yes, we know," Doc said.

"Is what he says true?" she asked.

"I don't know exactly what he told you, but if he said a man named Desmond Shaw is trying to kill him, he's telling the truth."

"We'd better hurry then. His men are all over this airport."

CHAPTER

Travis scurried along the mezzanine, frequently looking behind him to see if anyone was following. He wasn't sure whether Shaw's men had seen him, but he wasn't taking any chances. He walked as fast as his bum leg would allow without raising suspicion. Two policemen were standing at a counter talking as he walked past. He had no idea where he was in relation to the North Terminal, but he knew he had to get there somehow. A sign pointed downstairs to all connecting gates and terminals.

Glancing around furtively, he stepped on the escalator. Halfway down he saw airport security guards strolling past. Had they looked up they would have seen him. He was breathing heavily, and not just from exertion. When he got off the escalator, he flagged down the shuttle. "Excuse me; can you give me a lift to the next gate?"

"Sure, hop on. I'll take you there, but first I have to make a quick stop at maintenance to pick up some tools for the electricians."

Travis shed his security jacket and stepped onto the scooter.

The driver, an old man, guided the scooter off the main corridor and entered the Employee Only restricted area. He got off and entered the maintenance room, unaware that Travis had followed.

He hit the man over the head with his gun, gagged and tied him, and slipped a white airline maintenance technician uniform over his clothes.

* * *

Carter was on the overhead mezzanine when he spotted the odd looking driver with a backpack speeding down the main terminal. "Travis!"

Travis looked up and saw him. "Damn!" He pushed the accelerator to the floor.

"It's him! We have to get him." Carter shouted to the men below, and then radioed the others. "We've spotted Travis. He's in a shuttle, and he's heading north. Cut him off in the terminal before he gets to the north gate."

Travis was paying more attention to the men chasing him than the ones charging him from his left flank. He tried negotiating the right turn into the North Terminal, but turned too sharply. The scooter tipped over and slid into a tower of scaffolding.

"Get off with your hands up, Travis," said a guard.

Travis was still tangled in the scooter. From the observation window, he could see St. John's jet heading to the hangar directly across the runway. He looked around, but this time there would be no easy escape.

"I'm not telling you again, Travis. Get those hands up!"

Travis didn't have time to think. He raised his hands in submission. "Okay, I'm getting up, don't shoot."

At that moment, Carter and his men appeared from around the corner. The momentary distraction allowed Travis enough time to pull his gun and fire. Two men went down, and another was hit in the leg, but managed to crawl behind a row of newspaper vending machines. The other men took cover around the corner.

"How bad are you hurt?" Carter shouted to the wounded guard.

"Not bad enough for him to get by me."

"You hear that, Travis? You don't have any place to run. Give it up!"

Travis knew Carter was right. He was trapped.

●　●　●

Alexia was inside the airplane hangar when she got a call from one of her men. "We've got trouble over here. Those security fools are running wild and there's gunfire coming from the terminal."

"Lock it down. Lock down the whole airport. I don't want anyone coming in or going out. Find out who's doing the shooting and arrest them. I'll be there in a minute," she said.

"What's wrong?" Doc asked.

"We've got a problem and it sounds like it might involve Mr. Travis. I'm going to check it out and I want you and your party to stay here until I get back."

"I'm going with you," Doc said.

"No, you're not. You're going to stay here until I sort this out. I'll bring Travis to you. Just sit tight. I'll be back as soon as I can."

She hurried outside where her men waited. "We have a code red situation. I want this hangar secured and its inhabitants protected at all costs. If anyone other than the president of the United States tries to enter, I want them stopped," she ordered.

The large hangar doors slid shut, sealing its occupants into the metal tomb, as four heavily armed men stood guard at the entrance.

●　●　●

"We're going rush him," Carter said.

"You're out of your mind. There's no way I'm going out there and expose myself. We wouldn't have a chance; there's no cover," said one of the men.

"We'd better do something. Airport security will be here fast," someone else added.

While the men argued over what to do next, Travis had already made his decision. He knew he would have to act now while he still had the courage. There were only two rounds left in the Magnum and he couldn't afford to waste them. He needed another gun and the closest one was next to the dead guard—eight feet away. Travis crawled to the front of the scooter and used the straps from his backpack to lasso the gun and pull it to him. With sweat pouring down his face, he clutched a gun in each hand. His heart was beating faster than a racehorse runs and he tried to steady his nerves, waited a moment, and then sprang to his feet firing. The first bullet from the Magnum ripped through the newspaper box and lodged in the guard's chest. The second punctured the observation window.

Carter tried rushing him, but Travis fired four more rounds, repelling the men. By the time the guards regrouped, he had taken flight. He ran and hurled his body at the cracked observation window. The shattered glass sliced his flesh like a razor as he flew sixteen feet to the tarmac.

Travis's body hit the concrete like a rock. He lay on his back, writhing in pain, barely conscious and blurry-eyed—looking up at the astonished faces staring back at him. He tried moving, but screamed instead. His left knee looked like a crushed melon, but he somehow found the strength to fight through the pain and struggle to his feet.

Carter gaped down at him through the jagged frame of the shattered window as Travis looked up. For a second the two men stared at each other like poker rivals waiting to see who would make the next move.

Travis broke the standoff. He began to limp away, blinded by pain.

"I can't believe this guy. Where does he think he's going?" Carter asked no one in particular. Travis looked like a cartoon caricature dragging its body off to die.

Just then, Travis saw a red Cherokee speeding toward him. He began to hobble faster.

At the sight, something snapped in Carter's mind. Maybe it was the realization that he was about to lose to Travis or that someone else would get credit for his capture.

The car came to a screeching halt, and Alexia jumped out. She made Travis lean on her and helped him to the Jeep. As he tried to negotiate his way onto the seat, a single shot rang out. Travis screamed and fell against the open door. Alexia returned the fire and Carter tumbled head first to the ground.

"Get him in the car!" she shouted as she kept her gun aimed on the other men, who had lost interest in continuing the pursuit as they stared at Carter's body.

The driver pulled Travis's unconscious body into the Jeep as Alexia got behind the wheel and closed the door. "How's he doing?"

"He's still alive, but he's losing a lot of blood."

Alexia pressed the accelerator and raced to the hangar. The steel doors glided open to let her through. She pulled the jeep into a private parking stall next to St. John's jet.

"What's going on?" Marcus asked.

"Dana Travis is in the back. He's been shot."

Travis was motionless, lying face down on the seat in his blood-soaked maintenance uniform. Sydney went to get blankets and towels from the plane, while Doc cut the tangled backpack straps off his arm. Then they carefully rolled him onto his side.

Sydney propped the blanket under his head and gently wiped the blood from his lacerated face. Travis's eyes were closed and he was breathing hard.

The hangar door opened and one of Alexia's men entered. "We have a situation out here." Alexia saw flashing blue lights in the background. "The police are outside and they want to know if we have Travis in here. It's getting a little sticky. They want to talk to you."

Reluctantly, Alexia went outside. The runway was littered with blue and white police cars. She approached a pug-faced, fat man who stood at the front, glaring. "Are you in charge?"

"Yes I am," he said.

"I'm head of security at this airport. What do you want?"

"What do I want? You can start by telling your men to lower their damn weapons and then you can give me Dana Travis," said Kilgor.

⬤　⬤　⬤

Travis responded to the cool touch of the wet towel caressing his face. He opened his eyes and struggled to talk through his pain. He touched Doc's arm and whispered. "You're Sebasst?"

"Yes, save your strength. We're going to get you to a hospital."

"No hospital, can't go…can't let them get me…you promised."

Marcus stood watching the pathetic man. "We promised to help you if you told us the truth about the files, but you didn't."

"Had to get you here. That was the only way…"

"Well I'm here. You want my help? Then give me what I want."

"Backpack. Give me backpack."

Sydney lifted the backpack and emptied the contents. Intermingled in his clothes were a wallet, address book, and shattered pieces of a computer disc.

Marcus picked up some of the broken pieces. "Is this it?"

Travis shook his head.

"Then where is it?"

"Backpack…inside."

Sydney checked the zipper pockets, and didn't find anything. But when she moved her hand along the smooth nylon lining, her fingers touched a bulge in the corner of the flap, which had been neatly stitched. She punctured the lining with her fingernail and pulled out a key attached to a gold key ring.

"Is this it? What's it for?" Marcus asked. Only muffled noise came from Travis's mouth. "What? I can't hear you. What did you say?"

"Excalibur!" he wheezed as though it was his last breath, and then his eyes rolled.

"He out of it," Marcus said.

"Here, let me try," Doc said. He carefully lifted Travis's head off the blanket. "Listen Travis, what is this key to?" He dangled the key in front of his eyes.

"Phoenix 3126...6," he said.

"What?"

Travis tugged at Doc's shirt. "312 Phoenix Boulevard." He closed his eyes.

Marcus moved gingerly around the Jeep, trying to control his impatience and fear. If Travis died, this would all have been for nothing. "Is he dead?"

"No," Doc said.

Alexia re-entered the hangar. "How is he?"

"Not good," Doc replied. "He's too incoherent to tell us anything. He needs a doctor."

Alexia sighed. "I have to turn him over to the police."

"You can't!" Marcus blocked her way.

"I don't have any choice; they have a warrant for his arrest."

Slowly, Doc climbed out of the jeep, shaking his head.

"Sorry Julian. I have to let them take him into custody. If it makes you feel better, I'll ride with him to the hospital, just to make sure nothing happens."

"Thanks, but that won't be necessary."

❖   ❖   ❖

Kilgor watched the seconds ticking away on his watch. She had two more minutes to give up Travis or he and his men were going in. Just then, the doors opened and Alexia walked out.

The cops swarmed through the front of the hangar as a red Jeep left out the back. Travis's body was on the floor.

"I can't believe this. He's dead!" Kilgor shrieked. He had spent the last forty-eight hours tracking this man, and had come up empty. Then he noticed the backpack next to the body. Kilgor picked it up, discovered it was empty, and threw it as far as he could. "Did Travis say anything before he died?"

"I don't know," Alexia replied. She was calm and quietly confident, in sharp contrast to Kilgor whose face was purple with rage. "I was talking to you outside when he died."

"And the people who came in on that plane?"

"Gone."

"I can see that. Where did they go?"

Shrugging, Alexia murmured, "I don't know."

"And you just let them go?"

"They didn't break any laws."

Kilgor was furious. "They're material witnesses. For all we know they could be Travis' accomplices and you just let them walk away."

Alexia drew herself up straight. "Mr. St. John and his party received government clearance to land at this airstrip. Do you know what that means? When I get a call from Washington, telling me to provide priority one security for one of their people, I don't ask questions. If Mr. St. John and his party are involved with Mr. Travis; I suggest you notify the appropriate people in Washington."

She paused. "It's not my concern. As you reminded me so bluntly a few moments ago, my job is to provide airport security, not play policeman. Mr. St. John and his party did not violate any laws at this airport and consequently there was no reason to hold him."

Kilgor fumed, furious and powerless. He wanted to strangle the woman. Travis was dead, St. John was on the loose, and probably in possession of whatever dangerous information Travis had. Kilgor didn't want to be the one to give Desmond Shaw the bad news."

* * *

Leon-Francis's men arrived from San Diego on time. Their names, Woodberry and Morgan, had the magical ring of a prestigious accounting firm, and they looked the part, dressed in double-breasted suits. But that's where the resemblance ended.

Men wearing expensive clothing want to impress, be noticed, and most important, be comfortable. These two didn't fit the mold. Shaw could tell they were as uncomfortable in their matching ensembles as an ironworker in a tuxedo. Woodberry was the taller of the two, but both had impassive eyes that seldom blinked--especially Morgan. He didn't utter a word and never took his eyes off Shaw. They sat across from him in the limousine.

Shaw held out a bottle of scotch. "You fellas want a drink?"

"No," Woodberry said.

"You sure make a hell of an entrance in those matching suits and luggage. Is this standard issue clothing at Excalibur? If so, where do I sign up?" His attempt at humor was lost on them.

"We understand your cousin is in possession of information that may embarrass Mr. Leon-Francis," Woodberry said.

"How did you find out about that?"

"That's not important. We want to know what you're doing about it."

"Travis was apprehended by the police earlier today."

The men were obviously surprised and they exchanged a glance.

"Don't worry, he's dead. He was shot while trying to escape."

Woodberry leaned forward tensely. "Did he have anything on him? Because he's the one who broke into our system. He used his password and access number to log on. What we want to know is, what information did he get and where is it?"

Shaw's eyes widened and he shifted uncomfortably. "How would I know if you don't?"

"Was there anyone he could have passed the information to?" Woodberry persisted.

Shaw shook his head. "I doubt it. The man's been on the run for two days. If he had anything valuable, we would have found it on him."

"Why didn't you notify Mr. Leon-Francis about this?"

"I didn't see a reason to. I handled the problem."

Woodberry wasn't quite convinced. "Are you sure?"

"Absolutely," Shaw lied, wishing it was the truth. "Everything is back on track. You can tell Mr. Leon-Francis there's nothing to worry about." He became aware that Morgan's gaze had intensified. Shaw resented being interrogated like a common prisoner.

Woodberry also considered him in silence. "Good," he said finally. "Now that we have that straight, we have another issue to discuss with you. Mr. Leon-Francis is concerned about the Alpine campaign."

"Everything is fine on our end; we're on schedule. The morning newspaper has us up by twelve points and I think we'll increase the margin before election night."

The two men remained silent, so Shaw filled the vacuum. "Barring any last minute fumbles, Victor will win by a landslide. I already have a PR campaign ready to put into action once he's elected to the Senate. By the time he accepts the vice presidency, Victor Alpine will be a household name."

"Don't worry about the future. Mr. Leon-Francis has his own plans. Your responsibility ends the day he's elected. After that you'll be reassigned."

Shaw felt like he'd been kicked in the groin. "What do you mean?"

"Mr. Leon-Francis appreciates your hard work and diligence and you will be amply rewarded," Woodberry said coolly. "However, we are preparing to move to the next level and you are no longer needed here. You will be reassigned to a new project on the East Coast."

With an effort, Shaw had been keeping his low-boiling anger under control, but at that moment it erupted. "Reassignment my ass! In case you hadn't noticed, I'm not in anyone's damn army. I just can't pick up and leave; I've got too much invested here."

"All that you have belongs to Mr. Leon-Francis. You never owned anything except what he allowed you to keep. He considers you a man of immense talent and an asset to the organization. He would hate to lose your services over a disagreement such as this. You may want to rethink your position."

Shaw's burst of anger quickly faded and common sense took its place. He knew that disobeying Leon-Francis was not an option unless you didn't care about your life. "I'll do whatever he wants."

●　●　●

It was a forty-five minute drive from the airport to Anna's townhouse outside Seattle, where crime scene tape was still stuck to the door, along with a padlock. Marcus broke in the side entrance to the garage and raised the door for Sydney to pull Alexia's car in. Anna's boxes of personal belongings were still stacked neatly against the garage wall where Marcus had left them for her family. Sydney and Doc went to the kitchen to find something to eat. Marcus turned the television on and lay down on the couch. He was asleep in five minutes.

Sydney hadn't slept in thirty-six hours, but she didn't act like it. She removed everything from the refrigerator and spread it out on the counter. After slipping an apron over her white slacks, she proceeded to speed chop through the vegetables. When finished, she dumped the green onions, tomatoes, and mushrooms into the giant bowl along with six eggs and bacon bits.

Doc was on the phone with Asha. He purposely omitted telling her about the attack at Marcus's house and Dana Travis's death.

"We're at Anna's place. I'll probably be home in a couple of days. How's Carl?"

Asha laughed. "I haven't talked with him since he came and got your dogs. All he could talk about was the seaplane. The one thing we seem to agree on is that we love you. So be careful."

After the telephone call, Doc went back to the kitchen to see Sydney.

"I've never seen anyone with as much energy as you. Don't you ever stop working?" he asked.

She laughed. "Working with Marcus is a full time job. As long as I keep moving, I'm fine." She peeked around the corner into the living room and saw Marcus stretched out on the couch, snoring. "He's exhausted." Sydney folded the giant omelet into a frying pan, finishing it with a light sprinkling of seasoning salt.

"If you're expecting me to eat that, I think I'd rather take my chances with Shaw."

"Don't knock it until you try it." She sliced off a corner and fed it to him with a fork.

"I have to admit its pretty good," he said.

"Thank you." She smiled. "Was that your girlfriend on the phone?"

"Yes."

"What's her name?"

"Asha."

"Pretty name. Are you two going to get married?"

Doc chuckled. "Are you and Caitlin by any chance related?"

"Hey, I'm just asking—didn't mean to touch a nerve," she said as she placed a platter of food on the table. "It's generally what couples do when they've been together awhile."

Doc poured orange juice into three glasses. "How do you know how long we've been together?"

"I can tell by the way you talk to her. The softness and patience in your voice, and the way you artfully deflect her questions without overtly lying. You care a lot about her, and you worry that she worries about you. I've seen the symptoms before. That's why *I* choose to be alone. In this profession, I can't afford to be close to anyone."

"How did you get into this anyway?"

Sydney chose her words with care. "Some unfortunate

circumstances forced me to consider new career options. The personal protection field seemed like a natural fit for my abilities."

"That ornate Beretta you're carrying is issued by the Israeli secret service, Mossad. Did you work for them?"

She arched an eyebrow. "I can't talk about that."

Doc smiled. "Seems like I'm not the only one with secrets."

She handed him a plate and sat down. "You know the name Mohammed Karim?"

"Wasn't he the Jihad terrorist killed in Malta about six years ago?"

"Very good. His death was the result of an organized and efficient extraction process by the Israeli government and others."

"Which means you whacked his ass," Marcus said, yawning as he took a seat at the table.

Sydney passed him a plate. "We prefer to call it a caesarean. Over twenty agents were used, but I was one of eight personnel that played a crucial role in the mission. Shortly after Karim's death, Hamas vowed revenge. Over the next three years, five of our team members were tracked down and killed. For security reasons, the Israeli government thought it best that I leave the country. They eventually caught the assassin, but I never returned to Israel."

She noticed Marcus leafing through the photo album he had brought from the living room. Doc saw it too, but decided to let his friend reminiscence in peace.

Sydney turned to Doc. "Can I tell you something?"

"All of a sudden you need my permission to tell me what you think?"

A smile crossed her face. "You don't strike me as a person who ought to be teaching. Don't get me wrong; you've got the professorial look and I'm sure you're excellent, but I don't think it's what you were born to do. You're naturally gifted in other areas."

"Well I appreciate the flattery, but it was my so-called *gifts* that put me in my current position. Like you, I'd rather not revisit those times."

By the time they finished their meal, Marcus's head was sill in the clouds and he hadn't touched his food.

"Put the book down, Quik, and eat. You'll feel better."

Marcus closed the album. "I've been thinking a lot since we left the airport and, as much as I hate to admit it, I think we're out of our element here. You know I'm not one to run from a fight, especially when I know I'm right. But I just don't see how we can beat these guys. We're stuck in *their* city, 1,000 miles from home, with no resources and only the three of us. The police are working for Shaw, and as much as I hated Travis, he didn't deserve to die like that. They hunted him down like an animal, and we're their next prey. I'm sorry I let my ego and pride overrule my common sense and endanger you guys, but I think we need to pack it in and go home."

"You're not serious?" Sydney asked.

"As a heart attack."

"Did you forget that you'll have to constantly be watching your ass if you leave?" she asked.

"I'll take that risk."

"Marcus, what makes you think they're going to let us leave? We can't just go to the airport and fly out of here. We need to finish what we came here for."

"All we've got is this key and a bunch of mumbo jumbo from a dying man. We need more than that."

"Actually, we don't," Doc said. "Travis gave us the address; we just have to find the building and the object this key opens."

"Are you crazy? How do you expect to do that?"

"I don't know, but I'm willing to give it a try. There aren't many other options."

"You're a smart man, Doc, and I give you credit for getting us this far. If your warrior-princess lady friend Alexia what's-her-name hadn't helped us out at the airport, we'd be dead now. But luck can only get us so far. I can't believe you think we actually have a chance in hell of finding Travis's file."

"What I believe really doesn't matter. Sydney's right. Shaw isn't going to let us just waltz out of town. No way. And he's going to use all his power and every resource he has at his disposal to find and kill us."

"That's my point. If I still thought we could prove that Alpine and Shaw had Eve and Anna killed, I'd be willing to take the chance, but I don't. Travis has told us nothing but lies. Even if we find his so-called files, it probably won't give us the smoking gun we need."

"Even if we can't prove the murders, we can certainly bring Shaw and Alpine down. I'm not going to blow smoke in your face and tell you it will be easy, because it won't." Doc stopped to take a breath. "We can't make any more mistakes. This isn't the time to second-guess yourself. You want to stay alive? Then you need to stay angry because that's when you're at your best. Don't for a minute forget what they're capable of doing to your family."

"So, do you have a plan about where to start?" Marcus asked.

Doc pulled Travis's key from his pocket. "Right here with this key. Once we get some answers, we'll be ready."

"For what?"

"Payback. They've had their chances at bat and missed. They don't get a third shot. Now it's our turn."

CHAPTER

36

Asha was worried and it had little to do with her concern for Doc since he had reassured her that he was fine. For the past week she felt that something was wrong. There was an uneasiness she couldn't shake or explain that she tried ignoring, but that changed yesterday.

When she was swimming laps she felt that something or someone was watching her. Her anxiousness was heightened when she went for a stroll and found a clump of trampled West Indian Jasmines in the garden, by the pool. By the time she got to the restaurant, she'd convinced herself that she was just being paranoid.

Asha went upstairs to her office and paid some bills before going down to the kitchen to talk to the chef. The governor of the islands and her extended family were dinning at the restaurant tonight and she wanted to make sure that all the arrangements were ready. Jamal had reserved the north wing of the restaurant for the party. After ensuring that everything was in place, Asha headed back to the main room. She had to squeeze through a large crowd of people standing by the front door to get to Jamal.

"Have some more tables brought down. We can seat some of these people outside. They've been waiting too long."

"We may have space in the lounge," Jamal said.

"I'll check it out. You get the tables."

The lounge was also full, except for a few empty barstools. She walked over to the nearest table and introduced herself to her guests. One of the perks of owning a restaurant, and the thing she most enjoyed, was socializing with the patrons. She spotted a couple across the room—regulars, celebrating their anniversary. She flagged down a hostess and told her to send over a complimentary bottle of champagne.

"Aren't you gonna stop and talk to me?"

Asha looked down at the man attempting to grasp her arm. He looked like a retro-style detective in a novel, dressed in a white twill suit and bow tie.

"How are you, baby?" he asked with a Louisiana drawl.

It took Asha a few seconds to recognize him. When she realized it was Maurice Beale, she almost fainted. She grabbed the bar rail to steady herself. "What are you doing here?"

"Now that's no way to talk to your husband. You don't seem very glad to see me."

"What are you doing here?" she repeated.

"Just stopped by to see how you're doin', and check out how you invested our money. Looks to me like we did okay. Yeah, this place is real impressive. You've done a good job," he said, admiring the French chandelier suspended over his head.

"Get the hell out of my restaurant—now."

Beale's false smile disappeared. The pupils of his eyes widened, his neck veins reddened, and his jawbone was so tight it looked like it might shatter. Asha had seen that face before.

"Sit down or I'm gonna tell these people all about your pretty little thieving' ass. Now sit!"

A couple at the next table glanced over curiously. Asha gave a weak smile and sat reluctantly. "That's more like it. You know, Spoon was right; you still look mighty fine." He reached across the table, resting his fingers on hers.

She recoiled. "Take your hands off me."

"You know you still belong to me. There ain't nothin' that's going to change that. I still love you, baby, and I want you back."

"You must be out of your mind. I wouldn't go back to you if the devil himself were my only other choice."

He frowned, his eyebrows merging into a single dark line. "Fine then, let's talk business. I own fifty percent of this place and I want my cut, plus a return on my initial investment."

"I don't owe you a thing. This is my restaurant."

"I hate to differ with you, darlin', but in case you don't remember, we're still legally married—"

"We are not. I divorced you years ago."

Maurice smiled unpleasantly. "As I was sayin', we're married. Ain't no piece of paper changin' that. I own half of everything you got. Accordin' to my calculation, which amounts to a nice sum." He stuck his hand in his pocket and pulled out a piece of paper that was as rumpled as his suit. "Lets see. 'Bout $200,000, plus a piece of that fancy villa on the hill and, of course, this restaurant. Yeah, you have a pretty sweet deal cookin' here. That should make it about..." He scratched the paper with his pencil. "$1.8 million."

"You're crazy. I'm not giving you shit," she said, trembling.

"Oh my, now we use profanity. Is that what your esteemed professor taught you?"

Asha's mouth dropped open.

"You didn't think I knew about your lover, Dr. Julian Sebasst? Lives at 233 Divid, in St. Croix. I haven't seen the place myself, but my men tell me it's not impressive. I would've thought that a woman of your taste wouldn't stoop so low, but then again you were always gutter trash—until I took you in. But that's another story. I like the photo of you two he had on his piano—sweet. Think I'll keep it as a souvenir."

"You've been in Julian's house? Leave him out of this, this…"

Beale leaned back, crossing his arms over his chest. "That's real cute, darlin', defendin' the man you love and all. Maybe that's cuz your bookworm isn't much of a man." He had a wicked smirk on his face. "He can't defend himself, so you come to his rescue."

Asha let her anger get the better of her. "Don't think for a minute that you're even on the same level as him, because you're not. It's like comparing a mutt to a Dane. I pity you because you always wanted to be somebody important, but you ended up being nothing and that hurts. I see it in your face. I want you to leave."

Beale grabbed her wrist, twisted, and forced her closer to him. "I'm not goin' anywhere. In fact I'm thinking about relocating to this island paradise of yours. I'll hire me the best attorney money can buy and sue you for all you're worth. I'll spend the rest of my life makin' yours as miserable as possible," he snarled. "You and that dull-headed professor won't have a minute's peace after I tell everyone--especially the board of trustees at the university--who and what you really are. I'll cause so much trouble that a cockroach will think twice about eatin' at this place." He released her hand, pushing it away with distaste.

She massaged her wrist. "What is it you want?"

"I already told you what I want!" he said, slamming his fist against the table. He quickly slinked his arm around her neck and smiled for the people watching them. Then he whispered, "Now, now, it's not that bad. I'm feelin' generous tonight." He removed a handkerchief and dabbed the sweat from his face. "Tell you what I'll do. Give me a small token of appreciation for the years of alienated affection. Say…$300,000 cash, and we'll forget the whole thing. How 'bout it?"

"You're mad; I don't have that kind of money."

"Don't con me, Ezea. You're worth a helluva lot more than that. I want my money and I want it by tomorrow." He rose from the table. "Meet me tomorrow night in front of Hegerstone Gallery on the harbor at 11:00. Come alone, and bring my money or you'll find out I'm capable of a lot more than you ever imagined."

Asha sat alone—dazed. A few minutes later a gentle hand touched her shoulder.

"Are you okay, Miss Panther?" Jamal asked.

"I'm not feeling very well. I'll be going home for the evening."

"I'm afraid I have some bad news," he said.

She jumped to her feet. "What? Is it Julian, has something happened?"

"No, it's his house. It's on fire."

"What!"

"You can see the flames across the harbor." Jamal continued to speak softly. "A constable wants to talk to you. They're trying to contact Dr. Sebasst."

"And the dogs--what about his dogs?"

"Mr. Anderson has them, remember?"

"Yes, you're right, I...I forgot." The tears she had been holding back began to flow. "I have to go. Please take over for me."

Jamal watched her running up the stairs to her office then went to the bar and asked for the telephone. He called the Seawolf Cove. "This is Jamal; let me speak with Mr. Anderson, please."

  ⚫ ⚫ ⚫

Beale rode back to his hotel in a fowl mood. His reunion with Asha had not produced the response he had fantasized about. Instead of being the cowering and submissive girl he had known and loved, she was smug and defiant—traits he hated in women. But what really bothered him was the confidence he saw in those green eyes of hers when she spoke. She hated him, and now he hated *her* even more.

He took his anger with him to the hotel lounge where he tried to bury it in Caribbean Smoked Torches. The bartender passed him another oversized snifter filled with brandy and rum, swimming in liqueur and fruit juices. Most people couldn't handle one, but Beale was working on his third. The bartender watched him with amazement. Bigger men than Beale would have passed out by now. Except for a few slurred words that occasionally slipped from his mouth, Beale seemed completely sober. He had a gift for holding his liquor, but he was still an alcoholic.

"Can I get you anything else?" the bartender asked.

"Naw, not unless you can get me that whore."

The bartender looked around the room. "Whom are you referring to, sir?"

"You know the one I'm talking about, the one that thinks she's so uppity—Ezea or whatever she calls herself now. The one that's got you all fooled in believing she's a lady. Well, she's not. She was a low-down broke bitch when I met her and now she's just a rich one."

A woman sitting at the bar took her drink and moved to a table.

"Sir, you'll have to watch your language and lower your voice if you wish to remain in this lounge," the bartender said sharply.

"Fine. If you all want to continue kissin' her ass, that's fine with me. It don't make me no difference. I know what she is and where she came from. She wouldn't be anything without me. She owes me, you hear, she owes me!" he shouted. He snatched the brandy snifter and went to his room.

"What was that all about?" asked one of the guests.

"Beats me," the bartender said as he continued to wipe off the bar.

❋   ❋   ❋

Beale finished the drink in his room and flung the empty glass against the wall. He needed another one to make the pain go away, but no amount of alcohol could cure him of this suffering. He paced the floor in the small room, all the while twisting his fingers around his ponytail. Occasionally, he stopped to massage his temples. Inner voices raged war in his head.

He sat in front of a table covered in newspaper clippings, bank statements, and financial reports. The information was a culmination of two days of hard work by his men. A broken three ring binder held unintelligible scribbled notes on every bit of information he had collected on Asha and Doc. Every time his mind conjured images of them together, his headaches returned, followed by another bout of serious drinking. Between the alcohol and insanity, Beale never knew what was real and what was an illusion. The one thing he did know was that Asha's fairy-tale life was about to end.

CHAPTER

The next morning, Marcus emerged from the bedroom scratching his head. The living room was empty. He went into Anna's office where Doc was sitting behind the desk surrounded in paper. "Where's Sydney?"

"She went to get some food; she'll be back in a few minutes."

Marcus looked over his shoulder. "What are you doing?"

"Trying to make some sense out of this."

"Have you been up all night?"

"Yes."

"Any progress?"

Doc shrugged. "I can't figure out why those soldiers were killed on your property. It doesn't make sense unless someone wants us to get to Shaw and Alpine. It makes even less sense if it's Leon-Francis. I don't get it."

Marcus snickered.

"What's so funny?"

"You, bro. Just when I was damn near convinced you could part the Red Sea, I find out you're human after all. I tell you, it warms a brother's heart to see that you don't have all the answers," he chuckled.

"I'm glad to see you're in a better mood."

"I thought about what you said yesterday, and you were right. I don't want to spend the rest of my life looking over my shoulder. We've got to find a way to take these guys down. But I gotta tell you; you aren't making any points with me today. You don't look up to the challenge. In fact you look like hell."

Doc sighed. "Thank you for those kind words of encouragement. Now if you've finished cracking on me, maybe you're ready to do some work."

"Brother, take a break! You're not going to be any use to anyone if you don't stop worrying, and get some rest."

Sydney came in with a bag of groceries and a newspaper under her arm. "Since you're in the worrying mode, you might as well add this to the fire." She tossed Marcus the morning paper. "There's an article you're going to find interesting in there. It seems like the police are looking for two African-American males as possible material witnesses or accomplices of Dana Travis in the robbery at Venture Bank."

"Kilgor knows our identity; they could've just as easily included our names and photos," Marcus said.

"This way it's easier for them to shoot first, then ask questions," Sydney pointed out.

Marcus tossed the paper in the trash. "So what do we do now?"

"There's more to this story than Travis told us, I'm certain of that. He all but confessed to blackmailing Shaw over his parent's death. That I understand," Doc said. "And I buy his story that Shaw and Alpine killed Anna. I'm even willing to accept his conspiracy theory that Leon-Francis is using his money to maneuver Alpine into the White House. But I think Travis was onto something bigger than all that."

Marcus raised an eyebrow. "Hell, Doc, blackmail, conspiracy and murder? That's the trifecta. What can be bigger than that?"

"Don't know, but it's something. Why else was Travis spoon-feeding us information? I don't think he ever intended to tell us the whole truth—only the bits and pieces he wanted us to know. I'm starting to have my doubts whether his missing file is going to be any more useful than the one he gave us."

"Well, unfortunately," Sydney interrupted, "the incomplete file and key are the only tangible things we have to work with."

"I know. That's why I've spent all night pouring over the information we have, and discovered a couple of interesting things." Doc rummaged through the papers on the desk until he found a piece of Travis's broken compact disc. "Look at the label printed on the back."

Marcus turned the disc over in his hand. "*Audplaza Properties*. So what?"

"It's a small real estate company in Seattle. I checked their website and found they own some property a few miles from the airport. I think that's where Travis called us from the other night."

"I still don't get it."

"If you were running from Shaw and Alpine, wouldn't you want to take whatever information you had on them with you?"

"Sure, assuming it didn't weigh me down. What are you getting at?"

"I don't think Travis had any paper files."

"Well, if that's the case, we're screwed," Marcus said, tossing the disc on the floor.

Sydney said nothing. She was listening intently.

"Not necessarily. Take a look at this." Doc placed Travis's red address book in Marcus's hand. "There's nothing in that book except computer access codes and passwords. I think he accessed a computer network remotely and downloaded the information on the disc. It makes sense, and it's smart because he could access the files from anywhere in the world as long as he had a computer."

"Did you try using the codes?"

"I'd need access to the server and the name of the network. I don't know either, and Travis was smart enough not to record them in the address book."

"Then how are we supposed to find them?"

"I don't know. It would have to be a safe place—somewhere no one would think to look."

"How about his office?" Sydney asked.

Doc removed Travis's key ring from his pocket. "That would be too easy. Take a look at the key."

Marcus did so. The oval head of the brass-colored key was inscribed with a pentagram. "What about it?" Marcus asked.

"Now look at this."

Marcus looked at the sheet of paper in Doc's hand. "The designs are identical, but so are most pentagrams. Where did you get this?"

"Off Desmond Shaw's corporate website. It's part of his corporate logo, only this one doesn't have the sword. I think the key is from their corporate office in Evergreen."

"Whoa, hold on, bro. I see where you're heading with this. If you're thinking about breaking into Shaw's office building you better squash it."

"Travis gave us a partial address for the place we're looking for, and it's not Shaw's building."

"What partial address?" Sydney asked.

"There's no Phoenix Boulevard in Evergreen or Seattle."

"Travis wasn't making any sense before he died. Maybe he meant street instead of boulevard," Marcus said.

"I checked that out too, but came up empty. There is a Phoenix Avenue in downtown Evergreen, but the street numbers don't run as high as 31266."

"Maybe it's the number to an office suite, not an address," Marcus suggested.

"Possibly. I got a map of the downtown area off the Web. There are dozens of buildings and offices on Phoenix Avenue. We just need to find the right one."

"This is crazy, Doc. How do you know for sure you're right? And even if you are, how are we going to find it with the police crawling up our butts? I want to make sure where I'm going before I put my ass on the line."

"I'm working on it." Doc pushed a chair over for Marcus. "You may want to be sitting for this one. It's bad news."

"Humph, I'm getting used to hearing bad news coming out of your mouth. What is it?"

"I've been studying the pages of text we translated. Although it's incomplete, I haven't seen anything that implicates Shaw, Alpine, or Leon-Francis in anything."

Marcus glared.

"But remember Edmund Lawrence?"

"Yeah, that's the secret account Travis found in Shaw's books."

"Well, Travis's file includes a lot of financial records, transactions, and an investment portfolio owned by Edmund Lawrence."

"He told us he couldn't find anything on the guy. I guess that was just another lie."

"Yeah. According to Travis's information, Edmunds is a retired Seattle stockbroker who's invested heavily in annuities, stocks, treasury notes, and precious commodities. Based on what I've seen so far, the account is perfectly legal. There's nothing pointing a finger at Shaw, Alpine, or anyone else."

"I'm sick of this crap. Travis is dead and he's still got us jumping through hoops with his riddles," Marcus said.

Sydney was sitting on the floor, occupying her time going through the telephone book. "Travis was the senior accountant at Shaw Development, right?"

"Yes," Doc said.

"There's no listing for an accounting office in the book, but that's not unusual. Some businesses contract their accounting and billing services out of shop. Maybe Travis's office is offsite. If it is, we may find some clues there."

"It's worth a shot," Doc said.

Sydney picked up the telephone and placed the call.

The receptionist answered. "Shaw Development, how may I direct your call?"

"I was wondering if your billing office is located in your main building," Sydney asked.

"Our accounting department? Yes ma'am, I'll transfer you now."

"No wait, I don't want to be transferred, I just want--" Too late.

A friendly male voice answered. "Miller and Sheckfield Accounting, may I help you?"

"Yes, do you handle the accounting for Shaw Development?"

"Yes, we do."

"Where are you located?"

"Our office is on Pacific Avenue, downtown. How may I help you Ms...?"

"Aaah—Stuart, Mrs. Nancy Stuart." Sydney was making it up as she went along. "My husband recently passed away and I discovered through my attorney that he purchased several parcels of residential property in Evergreen some time ago. I'm in town for a few days and thought I'd take the opportunity to view the property. Unfortunately, in my haste and excitement to see my new granddaughter, I left the deeds on my coffee table. The only thing I can recall is that a Mr. Dana Travis signed the papers. Perhaps he might be available to show me the properties?"

"Mr. Travis is no longer with us, but maybe I can help. What was your husband's first name?"

"Nathaniel . . .Nathaniel Stuart II."

"I don't recall that name. Do you know when the property was purchased?"

Taking a breath, Sydney said, "About ten years ago, I think."

"Ten years? Well, that explains it. Our records only go back the last five years. We'll have to get the information from our other office."

"How long will that take?" She tried not to sound impatient.

"Maybe a few days. I'll have to do a little research first to determine if they're in our vault or archives center. Now you said that Dana Travis signed the deed?"

"Yes, I think that was the name."

"That's somewhat unusual since that wasn't his area of expertise. But of course that was way before my time. Let me do a little checking here." The phone went silent for a half a minute, before the man returned. "I can't find your husband's file anywhere. I'm going to have to check our archived records. They may be at our Records and Retention Center in the old Phoenix Boulevard Building. Why don't you give me a number where you can be reached and I'll give you a call when we find something?"

"Oh, don't bother. I'll call you in a few days before I leave town." Sydney hung up the phone. "You guys want to go for a little ride?"

•   •   •

The drive to downtown Evergreen took an hour and fifteen minutes. They followed the internet directions to the Phoenix Boulevard Building, located on Parkway Waterfront Park. The building was a fenced, three-story steel warehouse, suspended over the water at the end of a 400-foot pier.

"Damn, it looks like a floating city," Marcus said.

"More like a fortress," Sydney mused.

Marcus sucked on his toothpick. "If this place is a records and retention center, then Elvis and Sammy Davis Jr. are alive and kicking it together somewhere in Tupelo."

"Sydney, hand me my bag, please," Doc asked.

She passed him the duffel bag. He removed a small monocular telescope and surveyed the area. "You're right. This is more than an archive center. It looks like a fort, except I don't see any guards or personnel." He scanned the windows. "It looks empty."

"Let's check it out, then." Marcus was suddenly impatient.

"The gate's locked and there's no other access to the pier unless you want to jump in the water and swim over there. Just because we don't see anybody, doesn't mean it's deserted," Doc said.

Sydney peered upward. "Judging by the electronics I see mounted on the roof, I'd say they've got plenty of surveillance. There's no way anybody's going to come anywhere close to that building without being noticed."

"What do we do now? We can't just walk up to the gate and ask them to let us snoop around," Marcus said.

Sydney shook her head. "No, but the building looks like it's been remodeled recently. If we could get our hands on the plans, I can find a way around the security."

"The city's planning department may have a copy, but that means we have to go into the lion's den to get it," Doc said. "Unfortunately, it's across the street from the police department and downstairs from the mayor's office."

"We can forget that then," Marcus said glumly.

"As far as we know, the police don't have my description. I can go in while you wait in the car." Sydney sounded very determined.

"Too risky—too many damn cops around there. What do you think, Doc?"

"It is risky, but I don't think we have any choice. Sydney's right. We don't stand a chance of getting in that warehouse unless we can find a way to bypass the security. My vote's with her."

* * *

"Mayor Alpine, Mr. Shaw is here to see you," the secretary announced.

"Tell him to come in." Alpine folded his newspaper and tossed it on the desk just as Shaw bolted through the doorway, slamming the door behind him. "What's wrong with you?"

"I just came from another meeting with Leon-Francis's people. Those two give me the creeps, especially Morgan. He never says a word."

"But you told them--?"

"Relax. They're not worried about Travis anymore."

Alpine sighed in relief. "Any word on St. John?"

"We have an APB out on him and Sebasst. They can't hide forever. When they pop up, we'll get them both."

Alpine grinned.

"You sure seem in good spirits. You must have seen the latest polls," Shaw said.

"Yes, just now. We're going to win this thing, Desmond. With Travis out of the way, we can concentrate all our energy on the election. It's funny how things work out. A couple of days ago I thought my life was over. I was one step away from prison, and now I'm one giant step closer to Washington." He leaned back in his chair.

"This time next year I'll be vice president of the United States and you'll be there with me. I've been thinking of an appropriate reward for your loyalty and hard work. What do you think about being my press secretary?" Alpine beamed.

Pompous ass. You don't have a clue about what's happening. You won't be able to fart unless the mighty Leon-Francis gives you permission.

"Yeah, that's fine, Victor, but first things first. You have a bunch of reporters downstairs waiting to hear what you have to say about the teacher's strike. You're going to have to get the parties together and resolve this mess real quick. I don't want it to be an issue after you're elected."

● ● ●

Shaw and Alpine left the office together and walked across the hall to the waiting elevator.

"Good afternoon, Mr. Mayor," said one of the passengers.

"Hi, Kathleen, how's that son of yours doing?"

"Excellent. He left for the academy two weeks ago. Thanks again for all your help. I don't know what we would have done without your letter of support."

"I was glad to assist."

The elevator stopped on the fourth floor and five more people entered. The door closed and the elevator continued its descent. Alpine continued to talk, but Shaw became distracted by a young woman pressed up against him in the crowded space.

"Oops, I'm sorry," she said, accidentally hitting him with the long tubes in her arms.

"Not a problem. You must work in engineering?"

"How did you know that?"

Shaw pointed to the document tubes.

"I guess they *are* pretty noticeable. I hope I didn't injure you."

"I can't imagine you hurting anyone—unless it's a man's heart," he said with a smile. "My name is Desmond Shaw."

Before she had a chance to shake his hand, the elevator came to a stop on the second floor. "Nice meeting you," she said, "but this is my floor."

Shaw moved so she could leave, but couldn't resist watching her walk away.

"She's a looker, isn't she?" Alpine said.

"Yes, she is, but too young for you. Put your eyes back in your sockets, we've got work to do."

Sydney took the back stairs down to the first floor and out to the parking lot. Marcus and Doc were waiting in the car when Sydney came out. She opened the back door and slid in.

"How'd it go?" Doc asked.

"No problem. I got the plans and the original blueprints."

Doc was impressed. "How'd you manage that?"

"I took them when nobody was looking. You'll never guess who I bumped into in the elevator."

CHAPTER

When they arrived back at Anna's apartment, Sydney unfurled the large plans on the living room floor.

"The original Phoenix Building was a one-story fruit and vegetable canning plant back in the early 1900's. It closed during the Depression. Over the next twenty-five years, various companies used the building as a warehouse until the early 1960's when it was scheduled for demolition," Sydney explained.

According to the planning clerk, Desmond Shaw rescued it from destruction and planned to restore it as part of a waterway park redevelopment project. The problem was, there wasn't enough land near the waterway to create a suburban style shopping center. Shaw's only choice was to build vertically. He had added two new floors before he ran into opposition from the historic preservation people. They gave him so much grief over his plans that he eventually abandoned the project. The building sat unfinished and vacant until 1991, when he decided to lease it to Miller and Sheckfield."

Doc sat on the floor studying the plans. "What's this area over here? It looks like a bunch of hallways."

"It is. A series of connecting hallways and overhead walkways.

Shaw had them built to connect the individual stores to each other. Now the warehouse is filled with storage containers, archived records, and pallets of surplus office equipment."

"What's on the third floor?" Marcus asked.

"It's empty. Miller and Sheckfield only lease the bottom two."

"And security?" Doc asked.

"Their security electronics are top of the line and are hard-wired directly to the Evergreen Police Station. The layout of the electrical system and circuits is odd. Most service panels are located on the first floor or basement and not the top floor. Another thing; look at the wiring diagram here," she said, pointing. "They remodeled this place with a lot of high speed wire and circuits on the third floor."

"What for?" Doc asked.

"The original plan was to locate the security offices up there, but it was scrubbed when the renovation plans fell through."

Marcus rose to his feet and stretched. "And Shaw has never rented out the space? Looks to me like we need to start our search on the top floor and work our way down."

"That's assuming we can find a way in," Doc said, passing Sydney one of his cigars.

She smiled. "Thanks."

Marcus knelt and pulled out the second set of blueprints. They were eighty years old and rich in detail. "So these are the original plans for the cannery."

"Yes. I felt a little guilty stealing them, but they were too large to photocopy."

"How much of the original building is still intact?" Doc asked.

"The city's Historic Preservation Bureau made sure that the walls were preserved as much as possible. Only minor alterations to the windows and doors were made, but the interior was completely gutted." Sydney looked over the two men's shoulders at the plans.

"Hmmm. There was originally a loading dock in back of the cannery. Maybe we can get in from there," Marcus said.

"There used to be a dock, but it was torn down and the doors were sealed," she said. "The only thing back there now is water."

"Any accessible windows?" Doc asked.

"The windows are in front and back, and they're probably wired. It doesn't matter anyway, unless you're Spiderman. The nearest window is fifteen feet above ground and barely large enough for a small kid to crawl through. We can forget about a back approach."

"Then how about the roof?" Marcus asked.

"Impossible. There's no way to climb up without being spotted."

Marcus jerked the cigar from his mouth. "Damn, Sydney, you're making this hard!"

She threw up her hands. "I'm sorry, but whoever designed this layout had security in mind. The only way in is through the front door."

"Then that's what we'll have to do." Marcus was not about to give up. "It appears that we can sneak through the fencing here at the corner by the old icehouse, without being detected. It's about thirty yards or so between there and the cannery. If we can get that far, we may be able to disable their security."

Doc pointed to a spot on the old blueprints. "What's this area?"

Marcus and Sydney leaned over to get a better look.

"Looks like a trap door in the floor," Sydney said.

"Yeah, that's what it is. Canneries used them to dump their spoiled food directly into the ocean, but I've never seen one like this," Marcus observed.

Doc turned the plans around for a better look. "The trap door seems to be located in the first floor cellar, beneath the main structure. There's a connecting trough running from the cellar up to the first floor. The door may still be there."

"If it is, it's probably covered by a slab of concrete by now," Marcus said.

Sydney straightened. "Maybe not. Because of its historic significance, the city may not have allowed Shaw to touch it."

Marcus spun the prints around again. "Even so, it would be impossible to access unless you can swim, and I can't."

"The building is sitting on wood pilings. The plans show a water line elevation of six feet from the top of the water to the building. That's more than enough room to squeeze through in a boat," Doc said.

"A boat? How are we going to get a boat?" Marcus asked.

"The same way Sydney got these plans. Borrow it."

"Even if we're lucky enough to find the door, you know how difficult it would be to get it open, assuming it's not blocked? The floors of some of these canneries, especially the ones on the West Coast, were made out of eight-inch-thick oak stumps. Depending on the size of the trap door, it could easily weigh hundreds of pounds."

"You didn't happen to bring any plastique with you in your bag, did you?" Doc asked.

"You're crazy, Doc." Marcus scratched his chin and thought for a moment. "If you're serious about this, I can probably come up with something."

Doc stood up. "I think it's our best shot. If we can't find a way underneath, we do it your way."

"Fair enough, but we need some supplies, starting with a boat," Marcus said.

"That's easy," Doc said. "There are a half dozen boat rental shops on the waterway."

"And I need something a little more practical and less conspicuous than these boots and white slacks," Sydney told them.

Doc extinguished his cigar. "We'd better get moving; it's getting late."

Marcus couldn't hide his surprise. "We're going in tonight?"

"Yeah. I figure you've been sitting around long enough and are itching to get at it."

"You bet your ass I'm ready to get busy. One thing, we need to find an ammo shop."

"It's already on the list," Doc said.

CHAPTER

"Mr. Shaw, you have a telephone call on line two."

"I'm still in my meeting. Find out who it is and take a message," Shaw said.

"It's the mayor, and he says it's very important."

"Tell him I'll call him when I'm through." Shaw switched off the intercom.

Kilgor and the Colonel were relaxing on the sofa.

"Listen, I know you guys are pissed about staying out so long, but I'll make it up to you." He poured them another drink. "The last couple of days have been tough on all of us, especially you. Now that Travis is out of the way, we can relax a little."

"I don't understand why you want us to stop looking for St. John," Kilgor said as he lit another cigarette.

"Let the police catch them for us. You two don't need to take any more risks. The last thing I want is some smart reporter trying to make a connection between you and Travis. This has to be a police operation from here on out. Anyway, St. John's a moot point without Travis."

"I think you're making a mistake in writing these guys off. They're a couple of pit bulls and they're still dangerous," the Colonel objected.

"They could be anywhere out there. We can't afford the risk right now. Besides, I've got something else I want you to do for me. There are two men staying at the Sheridan Hotel I want you to follow. I want wiretaps, surveillance—the whole nine yards. Find out who they're talking to and about what."

"Who are they?" Kilgor asked.

"Woodberry and Morgan. Men I don't like. You don't need to know the specifics; just do what I tell you."

*   *   *

Shaw didn't leave his office until 9:30. He walked across the street to Grassi's for dinner, where his reserved table was waiting for him. The hostess handed him the menu, but he didn't bother opening it.

"Give me the chicken Alfredo, two slices of garlic bread, and a bottle of red wine. I'll take a dark beer while I wait."

A minute later she returned with his beer. Desmond unfolded his newspaper and started reading.

A man approached his table. "Mr. Shaw, how are you?"

Shaw looked up. "I'm doing well, Dale, have a seat."

The rotund man pulled up a chair. "I wanted to offer my condolences about Dana. I know how close you two were."

The man looked so serious, Desmond wanted to laugh. "Thanks, Dale, it was quite a blow to lose him. You want a drink?"

Dale declined the offer. "No, thank you. I'm here with the family. I saw you across the room and just wanted to stop by and say hi. I was just telling the wife all about Travis. Who would have thought a guy like that could rob a bank. He must have had some serious money problems."

"Yes, I guess he did. I wish I had known, I could have helped."

"I guess you never really know anyone completely, even your own cousin. I can't imagine *not* being able to make it on his salary. My family could live nicely on the kind of money he was making. Jeez, and he was single, too. Yeah, you never know. For instance, I never knew he worked in escrow."

The meddlesome black man was becoming annoying. Everyone who knew Dale Green knew you couldn't shut him up, once he got going.

"Travis never worked escrow," Desmond said in a cutting tone, hoping to discourage further conversation.

"That's what I thought," Dale continued oblivious to Shaw's impatience. "But this lady I talked to yesterday said his signature was on a real estate deed."

"She must have been mistaken. Travis only worked account receivables and billings."

Dale snapped his fingers. "That would explain why I couldn't find the documents she was looking for. She was convinced Travis had executed the papers." Dale scratched his chin in bewilderment. "I suppose she could have made a mistake. After all, she didn't have the original documents with her." It was clear Dale was not about to leave until this little puzzle was solved.

"Did you cross-check her name in the computer?"

"Yes, a couple of times. That's another thing that was strange. The system didn't show the name, and I couldn't find any records of the transaction."

"That's impossible."

"I know. So I was going to check the retention center to see if they somehow were sent there by mistake, but we got disconnected and she never called back."

"You told her about the retention center?" Shaw was becoming more uncomfortable by the second.

"I may have mentioned it. She was pretty insistent about getting the information."

"But she never called you back for it?"

"No." Dale had apparently begun to notice Shaw's anxiety. He blinked in confusion.

"Did she ask where the center was located?"

"I don't remember. Is there a problem?"

"It's probably nothing. In the future though, refrain from telling people where our accounting records are stored. For security reasons we need to protect the confidentiality of our clients. Now, if you'll excuse me, Dale, I have to make a business call."

"Yes, of course," he said as he rose from the table. He scratched at his chin again. "Sorry if I did anything wrong, Mr. Shaw."

"It's okay, Dale. Tell the family hello for me."

Shaw reached for his phone. "Kilgor, it's me. Look, you and the Colonel might have been right about underestimating St. John. Let's keep one of the teams out in the field until we catch them. Send some of the boys over to my house and Victor's for extra security. While you're at it, have some men stake out the Miller and Sheckfield Retention Center."

"You mean that floating tomb downtown on the water? What the hell for?"

"Just do it," Shaw said and hung up the phone. He was probably being paranoid, but he couldn't afford to take any chances. If anyone discovered what was really in the warehouse, there wouldn't be a place on earth he could hide.

●　●　●

Sydney sat in the living room watching television and cleaning her gun. Doc was on the phone in the kitchen and Marcus was busy working in the sink. Doc closed his flip phone and laid it on the countertop.

"Any luck yet?" Marcus asked.

"No, I can't reach either of them—Asha or Jamal."

"Well, don't worry about it. No news is good news. So now, Doc, what's up with you and your lady friend, Alexia?"

"What do you mean?"

"You know what I'm talking about. I saw how she looked at you."

"I thought you didn't like to pry into my business." Doc's tone was flat.

"I don't, but Caitlin thinks I need to be more humane, you know—act like I really give a damn about you. I'm just trying to improve my interpersonal skills, and get more in touch with my emotional side."

"And you think this subtle approach is going to get me to reveal my inner self to you?"

"No, like I told you, I don't care. I'm just being nosey."

Doc laughed. "Alexia and I are just good friends."

"That's pretty obvious. What else?" Marcus wiped his brow with his arm, being careful not to lower his hands. Doc grabbed a dishrag and dabbed the sweat from his face. "Thanks."

"Where did you learn to do this?" Doc asked.

Marcus carefully laid the cotton-soaked diesel fuel in a clay mold with ammonium nitrate. He finished packing the cavity with putty and gently sculptured it into a ball. When he finished, Doc placed it on the table next to the others. "Doc, I don't ask you to tell me how you know all the things you do. Don't ask me about my special skills," he said, smiling.

"Okay, but you're making me nervous with that stuff."

"Relax, I know what I'm doing. Hand me some of those over there."

Doc passed him the box. "At least take these off," he said, referring to the twin 45's holstered under Marcus's arms.

"Yeah, sure, take them. They're in my way anyway." Marcus raised his arms so Doc could reach them.

"They're nice," Doc said, laying the guns on the counter.

"A client gave them to me as a present a few years back."

"He must have known you had a lot of enemies."

Marcus laughed. "Yeah--I have my share. But I tell folks, don't start nuthin', won't be nuthin'. Now, before you get distracted again, I want you to tell me more about you and Alexia."

"You aren't going to let this rest, are you?"

"Hey, I'm doing all the hard work here. The least you can do is entertain me."

"All right, all right! We met in Europe a long time ago. I was in the Service and she was a naval officer with NATO. She's a good woman."

"And...?"

"Things just didn't work out. We moved around too much. When I was in Madrid, she was in Stuttgart. When I was in Germany, she'd be stationed in Poland, Norway or Greece somewhere. We never seemed to be in the same country together, much less the same city. We were in the wrong occupations for a relationship to work."

"Well, she's definitely fine. I don't understand how an old fart like you could pull someone that good looking. I guess you're living proof that opposites do attract. You know, like beauty and the beast."

Doc waved him off. "You're an idiot. I don't know how Caitlin puts up with you."

"She can't help but love me, just like you can't. I'm so pimp delicious I can't stand myself!"

Sydney appeared in the doorway. "Aren't you guys finished yet?"

Marcus carefully placed the last explosive in the gym bag. "Almost." He zipped the bag and retrieved his guns. Doc and Sydney went down to the garage to get the car.

Marcus took one last look at the flat. "Payback time, baby." He turned the lights off and closed the door.

Two minutes later, Doc's cell phone rang with Jamal Calderon's name displayed across the screen, but Doc was already gone; the cell was still sitting on the kitchen counter where he'd left it.

CHAPTER

Maurice Beale slumped in his chair, sullen and depressed—and still seething about his disastrous meeting with Asha. His desire for her was now dead, killed by her acid remarks, and now he hated her more than ever. He had something special in store for her. But that would have to wait until after he got his money tonight. Spoon came into the room with Beale's suit jacket draped over his arm.

"The boys ready yet?" Beale snarled.

"They're waiting in the car. You?"

Beale nodded. "Remember what to do when we get there?"

"Yes, but boss, don't you think it's a little excessive?"

"*Excessive*? The woman doesn't deserve to live. She destroyed my life. When I'm through with her, she'll beg me to kill her, but I won't. I want her man to see her like that. Then we'll find out if he still wants her. I wish I could be here to see his expression when he comes home and finds what's left of his house and whore." Beale was like a rabid dog out of control. The only difference was he hadn't started foaming at the mouth yet.

"Come on, boss, you don't wanna be late." Spoon helped him put on his jacket.

Killing Quick

* * *

The Hegerstone Gallery was located at the end of the pier. Beale found Asha waiting for him when he arrived.

He cautiously looked around to make sure she was alone. "Where's my money?"

Asha opened a bag, pulled out a large yellow folder, and handed it to him.

Beale ripped the folder open and pulled out a stack of money. He didn't need to count it. "What are you tryin' to pull? There's only about fifty grand here."

"Actually, $43,850: $23,500 plus interest. If you really believed I'd give you my hard-earned dollars, you're crazier than I thought. I admit you scared me when I first saw you, but I'm over that. You'll never have power over me again. Your bullying tactics and threats don't work anymore. If you want to tell the world about me, go ahead; I won't stop you. I don't care what you or anyone else thinks of me; it's not going to change who I am or the quality of my life. But if you even think about trying to shake me down or take anything of mine, my attorneys will fight you in court until that greasy ponytail of yours falls off."

Beale felt like his head was spinning out of control. "I want the rest of my money Ezea!" he hissed.

"You have the only money you're getting from me. Consider the balance owed your donation to the Julian Sebasst Building Fund."

The words stung like fire. Beale swung out, hitting her with all the power his small frame could muster. She flew off her feet, hitting her head on the pier.

Minutes later she opened her eyes to discover she had been dragged to the back of the gallery. Three men stood over her. "Get her up on her feet!" Beale yelled.

One of the men grabbed her by the waist and lifted her effortlessly off the ground. Her knees buckled.

Beale hit her again, knocking her unconscious. They revived her again, and Beale jammed an oil-soaked rag into her bloody mouth. Both her eyes were swollen shut."

"Now, you're finally gonna get what you deserve. I'm gonna start by givin' you something to go with that souvenir you already have on your neck. Then I'm going to carve up the rest of that pretty face of yours—real slow. When I get done, I'm gonna let my boys have some fun too."

Asha heard the blade disengaging from Beale's switchblade. The slits of her eyes filled with terror at the sight of the six-inch stiletto as he placed it against her neck. Her body convulsed when the blade dug into her skin, her muffled scream going unheard.

A large blurry object flew past Asha's eyes, devouring Beale's hand. He screamed and fell to the ground. Another beast attacked one of the men holding her, locking its jaws on the man's face. Beale thrashed around helpless as the dog chewed his hand. Somehow he made it to his feet, but that was a mistake. The dog released his arm and attacked his crotch. Beale howled.

One of his men watched the carnage and decided he had seen enough. He released Asha and ran—right into Jamal Calderon' s baseball bat.

Carl Anderson appeared from the shadows, wielding a steel pipe. He swung it at Spoon's stomach. Spoon dropped to his knees, and Carl smashed the pipe against his head.

Then Carl picked Asha up off the pier and carried her to a boat tied nearby. "Come on, boy, we got to get out of here!" he said, gently placing her body on the cushioned bench.

Jamal untied the anchor rope and jumped in as Carl removed the rag from Asha's mouth. "Miss Asha?" She was still unconscious. "Sabu, Taurus, here boys. Come!" Carl shouted.

The two Great Danes broke away from their attack, ran down the pier, and jumped onto the moving launch. "Good boys," he said, rubbing their heads. "Let's go, mon."

Jamal eased the launch away from the dock and puttered out to the harbor. Asha woke when she felt a wet towel on her face.

Carl grinned at her with his gap-tooth smile. "You rest. You'll be all right, no broken bones." She turned her head and saw Jamal steering the boat.

He read her mind. "I knew you were in trouble, so I called Mr. Anderson."

Asha managed to raise her hand and touch Carl's weathered face. "Thank you…" she whispered.

He grinned and gently laid her head back down. "You rest now. Anyway, Taurus and Sabu do the hard work, mon."

The dogs nuzzled their heads against the old man's legs when they heard their names.

CHAPTER

Shaw consumed more wine than linguini. He was more preoccupied with his future than he was with feeding his hunger. The wine helped him face the stark and painful reality that Leon-Francis no longer had a use for him. He knew he deserved a better reward. After all, Victor Alpine would be nothing if Shaw hadn't shaped, molded and polished him into the quintessential politician. But now all his hard work had been in vain. Instead of sharing in the future glory and power with Victor, he was out--just like that. "I'm not going out like that!" he muttered.

He felt good about the decision as he left the restaurant and walked backed to his office. Shaw was usually a cautious and deliberative decision maker, but the wine had empowered him with a new boldness; he would take control of his own destiny. It was time to get out and take his money with him. He would miss the black marble building he had erected as a monument to himself and the power that came with it. But with the money he would be taking with him, he could buy anything he wanted. Best of all, he had found a way to beat Leon-Francis at his own game.

Shaw entered the quiet lobby and took the elevator up to his office.

There were two messages from Alpine. As much as he hated returning those calls, he knew Alpine could buy him some extra time.

"Sorry to wake you, Victor, it's Desmond."

"Yes, I just wanted to run some ideas past you concerning the teacher's strike."

"Of course, but we can talk about it later. Right now I've got to get some sleep. I have a big joint venture deal closing in California, and I'm catching an early flight in the morning. I'll be back in a few days."

"A few days!"

"Relax, I'll make it back in time for the benefit. See you when I get back." Shaw hung up the phone, then went on the Internet and booked a one-way ticket to Miami with a connecting flight to the Bahamas. The only thing he had to do now was clean out the office and pack up a few things from the house.

He spent the next hour shredding sensitive and confidential documents to cover his tracks. When finished, he opened the mini-refrigerator, pulled out the ice tray, and unlocked the safe hidden in the freezer. Inside were two stacks of cash, a passport, and a small wooden jewelry box. He placed the items on the bar and poured himself a shot of bourbon. He opened the passport containing his picture, but with a different name: Edmund Lawrence. Shaw smiled and placed the passport in his pocket. He drank the shot of bourbon and opened the jewelry box. It was empty.

"What...! Where is my key?" He searched frantically through the few items still in the safe, but it wasn't there. He looked in the desk drawers and the closet, but still no key. He sank down in his chair in disbelief.

It's the alcohol....key has to be here. Got to think. He pulled out the spare key he always kept on his body. There was no way he could have lost the original because it was always kept in the safe. As impossible as it seemed, there was only one explanation. It had been stolen. No one knew about the existence of the safe, much less the combination number. Desmond thought about the people who had access to his office.

"Oh, no!" He fumbled for his desk phone. "Kilgor, get the boys and meet me down on the waterway at Miller and Sheckfield, *now!*" He threw the phone down, grabbed his gun from the desk, and ran downstairs to his car.

Leon-Francis's men, Woodberry and Morgan, sat across the street in a rented car, watching Shaw's Lexus peel away from the curb. They started the car and followed.

● ● ●

The bolt cutters easily snapped the gate chain to Jerry's Marine and Boat. Soon three dark figures eased black kayaks into the water and pushed off from the dock. They paddled slowly down the waterway, being careful not to create any noise. They seemed invisible on the black water.

Doc and Sydney manned the lead kayak with Marcus following closely behind in the other. The silver building lay 600 yards ahead, suspended in the air on black pilings. Doc slid the boat under the structure and grabbed onto a post. Marcus pulled alongside.

Sydney turned on the flashlight and studied the map. "It should be over here."

She pointed and they paddled farther underneath. The stench of the barnacles mixed with the smell of tar and rotten wood was overpowering. Sydney coughed at the pungent odor.

"We better find it soon, before the smell kills us," Doc whispered.

The kayaks weaved in between the endless pilings for what seemed like an eternity. It was worse than looking for a needle in a haystack; they were looking for an irregular seam amongst 97,000 square feet of rotting timbers.

"I think I might have something," Marcus said.

Doc and Sydney rowed over to him. "Up there. Shine the light."

The beam revealed a sunken section of flooring seven feet directly above their heads.

"That's it," Sydney said.

Doc hoisted himself onto the truss, braced his weight against the wooden frame, and used his long legs to push against the door. It didn't budge. "We'll have to blow it."

"Let me up there," Marcus said. He climbed up the sappy post and held on to the truss for support. "Give me one of the devices out of my bag."

Doc handed him a clay ball, which Marcus attached to the middle of the door and pulled out his lighter. "Get out of the way; I don't know what this thing will do." Doc moved the kayaks behind the pier post.

Marcus lit the fuse and shielded his body from the blast. Five seconds later it exploded with little noise, and no damage. "Damn, hand me some more." He placed charges in each corner of the door and lit them in tandem. The explosion sent Marcus and the 300-pound door down into the water.

"What the hell was that?" a guard standing on the pier asked.

"I don't know, but I felt the ground move. It sounded like an explosion. Check it out," said the other guard.

The man ran over to the edge of the pier and looked over. "I don't see anything."

Doc reached underwater and pulled Marcus into the boat. "You okay?"

"I think so."

After making sure, Doc shimmied up the post and pulled himself through the giant hole in the floor, then reached down and pulled Sydney up. The room was cold and dark, with wooden timbers substituting for walls and a ceiling. The only light was the moon's reflection on the water, shining through the hole in the floor.

All three turned on their flashlights. Directly in front of them was a massive wooden door, which was sealed. Marcus set another charge, blowing it off the rail. They ran up the concrete ramp leading to the first floor.

    ●   ●   ●

Shaw met Kilgor and the Colonel at the gate, followed by four Suburbans filled with men. Desmond honked his horn for the guard to unlock the gate.

"Mr. Shaw, is anything wrong?" the guard asked.

"Has anyone been here?"

"No, but we heard some kind of explosion just now. We're checking it out."

"Hey, over here," shouted another man. Off the side of the pier, a black kayak banged against the rocks. "That wasn't here a minute ago."

"They're here," Shaw said, teeth clenched.

"Who?" Kilgor asked.

"St. John and Sebasst, you idiot. They're in the building!"

    ●   ●   ●

Marcus stood staring at the endless labyrinth of intersecting hallways and corridors. The first floor of the warehouse was covered with forty-foot long shipping containers, crates, and pallets holding surplus office equipment—all neatly stacked in twenty-two -foot high columns. "Now I know what a rat feels like when he's looking for the cheese. How are we supposed to find anything in here?"

"Which way do we go, Sydney?" Doc asked.

She examined the map in her hand. "The elevator is on the northeast side of the building--this way."

    ●   ●   ●

The nervous guard fumbled with the key as he tried to open the front door.

"Give it to me, you fool," Shaw snapped. He opened the door and deactivated the silent alarm. "I don't want the police snooping around until I'm sure they're dead. Take the men, spread out. I want this entire building checked, and if you find anything moving, kill it. I know they're here."

Kilgor separated the men into two groups and hurried off.

Shaw waited until they were out of sight before ducking behind a row of boxes against the wall and disappearing up the hidden staircase.

Doc was the first to hear the voices. "We've got company and they're heading this way. He looked up at the column of steel storage containers, each of which had a foot ladder at the end. "We can hide on top of the containers." They started climbing, but three quarters of the way to the top, Sydney's hand slipped off the ladder, dropping her onto a stack of pallets, which crashed with her down to the floor.

Kilgor stopped. "What's that noise?"

"It came from over there," the Colonel said.

Doc jumped down and lifted a wooden crate off Sydney. "You okay?"

"Yeah, thanks."

Marcus reached the top—just in time to see a stream of men running through the maze toward them. "Fools at 2:00 coming hard. Come on, Doc, move your ass. The bad guys are here," he whispered.

Three men came up from the left, while the Colonel's men converged from the right. Marcus drew his guns, but kept his eyes fixed on both groups.

Doc hoisted himself up, but Sydney was struggling to reach the last ladder rung. "Help her up, Quik."

"Kinda busy right now, brother." The first wave of men turned the corner. Marcus's guns exploded, and two men fell. The guards spotted him, and open fired.

Doc hoisted himself up, pulling Sydney with him. Two men fired, but missed. Marcus pivoted and emptied his guns on them. A bullet passed over Doc's head. He turned and shot the man approaching from the overhead container. Another guard popped up and Doc shot him down. Then came another and another, until men were swarming everywhere.

"Looks like these people really don't like you," Doc said as he kept firing. Marcus ejected his spent clips, jammed two new ones in, and began firing again. Doc looked around for Sydney but she was gone. Somehow she had managed to make her way across the tops of the containers to the wall and back down to the floor. Doc saw her crouched behind a girder.

Marcus saw her too. "What the hell does she think she's doing?"

"She's trying to reach the elevator; cover her!" Doc shouted.

Sydney rose to her feet and heard the staccato gunfire following her. She leapt over a crate, took cover behind a desk—and waited. When the guards refocused their attention on Doc and Marcus, she sprinted to the elevator.

"I'm open to any ideas you've got, Doc."

Doc spotted Sydney signaling him from behind some boxes. Pulling another clip from his waist, he reloaded. "Sydney found the elevator, we have to go!"

Marcus ducked back behind a crate. He glanced over to see how far away she was. "There's no way in hell we're going to make it way over there without those guys reaming us a new butt hole."

"We don't have a choice, unless you want to stay here until you're out of bullets."

Marcus looked in his bag. He had one clip and one explosive left. "Okay, but you go first. I'll keep them busy."

"Are you crazy? I'm not leaving you up here by yourself."

"I've got more ammo—you go first. I'll be right behind you. Go!"

Meanwhile, the men were inching their way closer.

No words passed between the friends, but their expressions revealed that everything was not going to work out as they had hoped. Marcus retrieved the last explosive from his bag.

Doc looked at him. "Your ass better be right behind mine."

"It will be, bro, just get going, I've got your back."

Doc took a deep breath. "Ready?"

"Anytime."

"Now!"

Marcus lit the fuse and threw the clay explosive at the pile of surplus metal desks in front of the men. The explosion showered the area in metal shrapnel.

Kilgor staggered to his feet, wiping blood from his face. He turned around and tripped over a protruding desk leg—impaled in the Colonel's neck. Kilgor gagged and stumbled backwards. He saw Doc running across the top of the overhead container.

"Get him, shoot!"

Three men had an angle on him, but Marcus's bullets repelled them back behind the crates. Doc leapt down to a wooden crate, and bounced to the floor. He grabbed Sydney by the hand and they ran for the elevator.

"Where's Marcus?" she asked.

"He's coming."

Marcus peeked up to see how far he had to go, then fell back behind the box and wiped his brow with his sleeve. An eerie quietness set in as everyone waited to see what he would do next. He caught his breath, jumped up and ran toward the elevator with both guns firing. He took a hit and disappeared between the crevices of two containers.

Sydney screamed his name.

Doc grabbed her by the waist and pushed her into the elevator. "Hold the elevator. I'll get him!" He hurdled over a stack of archive boxes and ran down the aisle.

Kilgor looked up at Marcus's limp body dangling eleven feet in mid-air, wedged between the containers. "Pull him down from there."

The men climbed up on pallets and yanked him down by the legs. Marcus's body crashed to the floor. "He's alive, turn him over."

Marcus opened his eyes and saw the puffy-faced man leering at him. "St. John, good to see you again." Kilgor stomped on Marcus's shoulder, and he groaned. "Tough guy, huh? You should have kept your nose out of our business."

"You should've taken your fat ass to Jenny Craig."

Kilgor kicked him. "Looks like you and your buddy went through a lot of trouble for nothing—just like your reporter friend. You see where that got her."

Marcus made a feeble attempt to reach the gun on the floor. Kilgor kicked it away. "Get him up on his feet."

Gunshots reverberated through the warehouse and three guards fell. Two more shots and two more guards.

"Take cover, take cover," someone yelled. Marcus crawled underneath a desk. He tried reaching his gun, which was lodged between two columns of pallets. A strong arm found his hand and dragged him through to the other aisle.

"Looking for this?" Doc whispered, handing him the gun.

"Thanks. It's good to see you, man."

"Likewise. Can you make it?"

"How far?"

"Forty yards, Sydney's got an elevator waiting for us."

"Where are the bad guys?"

"On the other side, circling the wagon. It won't be long before they discover I'm not there."

"Does anyone see him?" Kilgor shouted. The men mumbled to each other, but no one answered. "Fan out, find him!"

"Let's go," Doc whispered. He pulled Marcus to his feet and draped his injured arm around his neck. "Ready?"

Marcus nodded.

Doc ran, dragging his friend as he went. They took cover under the stairs. "The elevator is just around the corner. We've got to do this before they find us."

Marcus nodded again. He was getting weaker. "You stay behind me. Come on," Doc said. They stepped out from beneath the steps. Neither saw the men charging at them from behind.

Sydney suddenly appeared. "Get down!"

Doc pushed Marcus to the floor as Sydney fired. Two of the men fell and the others dispersed. She and Doc helped Marcus off the floor and ran with him to the open elevator. Doc hit the elevator button for the third floor. Sydney propped Marcus up against the wall and inspected his wound. "How's the pain?"

"I've been better. I sure as hell hope there's another way out of here. I don't want to have to go out the same way we came in."

When the elevator reached the third floor it stopped, but didn't open.

"Is it stuck?" Sydney asked.

Doc pushed the button, again, but the door didn't budge. "No, it just won't open. There's something strange going on here." He pushed the "open" button repeatedly, but the door still didn't move.

Marcus fought to keep himself braced against the wall. "You'd better figure out something fast, Doc. We can't go back down there." Suddenly, the elevator jarred loose and started moving--down.

"No!" Sydney shouted.

"Someone overrode the system!" Doc hit the second floor button just in time. The elevator stopped and the door opened. Before he could step out, a bullet ricocheted off the elevator door. "Get back," he yelled.

The guards were fifty feet away and closing. Marcus was an easy target, clinging to the handrail. Sydney pushed him behind the door panel as a burst of gunfire slammed her body against the back of the elevator. Doc shot the gunman, and frantically hit the elevator buttons. The door finally closed and the elevator began its slow ascent back to the third floor.

Marcus was sprawled on the floor holding Sydney's head. "She's hurt--real bad!"

Doc looked down at Sydney's bloody body. There wasn't anything he could do for her or his friend. There wasn't enough time. The elevator came to a stop on the third floor, again, with the same results. The door didn't open. Doc frantically pushed the open button. Time was running out. He opened the service panel box and yanked out the wires, which short-circuited the elevator. He forced his fingers between the door panels and pried the doors open.

The third floor looked like the inside of a metal warehouse. The walls made of corrugated sheet metal and the arched rafters were made of steel. The floor was empty. Doc listened for the sound of footsteps, but there were none. He dragged Marcus and Sydney out of the elevator and laid them on the floor.

Marcus was covered in Sydney's blood. He tried to sit upright against the wall, but couldn't. "You're wasting time, man. You can't help us."

"I can't leave you here by yourselves."

"It won't matter if you can't find a way out of here," he said, looking around at the empty space. He coughed and grit his teeth. "Man, I can't believe this place is empty. We did all this shit for nothing."

Doc stood up. He couldn't believe it either, but he trusted his instincts, and they told him he was missing something. He walked around the open space looking for anything—a matchbook on the floor, something other than a layer of dust. He headed back towards the elevator, noticing there weren't any stairs, which didn't make sense. There had to be another way off the floor. He found something else odd. Directly across from the elevator on the wall were a row of electrical gauges, switches, and utility boxes. That's when it hit him.

He remembered seeing a diagram of a security room on the warehouse blueprints located on the third floor. He surveyed the room again, but this time he noticed something next to the utility boxes. He moved his fingers slowly across the corrugated steel wall; where he felt, but could barely see, two vertical lines running from the floor to the ceiling—one on each side of a locked utility box. Doc checked his gun. He had only two bullets. He stood back, shot the lock off the hinge of the box and raised the lid.

"Damn." He found himself staring at a fifteen-key digital lock and key slot. He punched in the numbers 31266, given to him by Travis, and then pulled the key from his pocket. He slid the key in the slot and turned. Behind the wall, he heard the electronic locking pins retracting. He lightly touched the wall with his fingers and the door slowly rolled back on its ball bearing hinges. Doc cautiously entered the lighted chamber.

A row of eight surveillance monitors was framed along the circular wall. In the middle of the room was a raised steel platform with a computer console and a Honeywell Server. Shaw was sitting at the consol, pointing a gun at him.

"This would have been a helluva a state-of-the-art control center, if the city would have let me open this place, but that's another story." Shaw saw the gun in Doc's hand. "Let it drop."

Doc released the gun.

"The name is Desmond Shaw. Which one are you?"

"Sebasst."

"That's a shame. I was looking forward to meeting Marcus St. John."

"I see you've been entertaining yourself at everyone else's expense."

"Too bad they didn't get you, but then again if they had, we wouldn't have this opportunity to share. I'm impressed by your persistence."

Doc spoke calmly, though he wanted to scream. "I'd rather you were dead."

"I think you have something of mine."

"What?"

Shaw's expression turned serious. He didn't have to ask again. Doc moved his hand toward his front pocket.

"Very slow," Shaw said, keeping the gun trained on him. Doc removed the key and tossed it over. Shaw inspected it and seemed satisfied.

"In about five minutes the police are going to storm this building and you're going to have a lot of explaining to do about those dead men downstairs."

"By the time they find the stairs up here, you'll be dead and I'll be gone." He stood up and walked around the end of the console.

"Before you go, tell me something. Why did you kill Eva Ward?"

"Actually that was the one thing I didn't approve. Victor was running scared because she had become a pain in his political ass. He needed control of the city's political machine in order to establish a power base. In order to do that, we had to bring in our businesses. Victor was convinced it wouldn't happen as long as Eva was alive, because she didn't support the kind of aggressive redevelopment we wanted, so she had to be dealt with."

He paused. "Given some time and money, we could have moved her out, but Alpine was too impatient. He wanted her dead. Who was I to argue with him? Once she was out of the way, we eventually took over. With Victor as the head of the Planning Commission and me the president of the Downtown Business Association, the rest was easy. The city was approving my development proposals faster than ragweed growing. Everything after that was easy. We decided what businesses came in and what ones we could trust. When Victor first ran for Mayor, our political machine was in its infancy and we made some mistakes--mistakes that almost got us caught. The mayoral elections taught me the most important lesson to be learned in this game of corruption and deceit. Would you like me to tell you what that is?"

There was a silver glint in his eyes. He was in his element and desperately wanted to share his genius with someone. And Doc needed to buy some time. "Why don't you tell me," he said sarcastically.

"The key is to grease *all* the skids, not just some. We almost got caught in 1995, because a smart bank examiner found some discrepancies in one of our business accounts. At the time, I was only paying off a handful of local politicians and cops. I'd forgotten about the 'little' and 'middle' man—the people in the chain that can screw everything up.

"I learned a valuable lesson. Moving and washing money is like oiling a chain; the beauty of the system is that I'm the only one who knows who they are and how everything fits together. Everyone else, including Victor Alpine, is just a link on the chain. They are only told what they need to know, and as long as I'm feeding them cash, they're happy and quiet." Shaw beamed.

"Everyone except Dana Travis. Seems like your infallible chain has a few chinks."

The smile disappeared. "My one regret is that I didn't kill him when I had his father killed. He was one sick puppy."

"And I guess you think your boat floats to the top."

Shaw smirked. "I bet Travis didn't tell you he helped get rid of your sister. He watched her be killed, then helped throw her body in the incinerator in the basement of the building. Travis bagged the bones and tossed them in the bay. He really got off on it."

Doc fought to maintain his composure. "How did she die?"

"Let's just say the killer had a passion for his profession."

"Who was he?"

"He flew in, did the job, and left. I never knew the name. We contracted the services through one of Leon-Francis's people--a low-life loser named Beale. He set up the deal."

"Maurice Beale?"

Shaw's face registered surprise. "You know him?"

Nausea almost overwhelmed his stomach, but Doc didn't flinch. "Our paths have crossed."

Shaw laughed. "Well, what a small world we live in. If you had the misfortune of running into that psycho, it couldn't have been good. You really aren't having a good day are you?"

"I'd say Travis didn't bring any sunshine into your life either. Why did he turn on you?"

"I don't know what the *hell* came over him. He was making money like everyone else, more so because he was always putting the squeeze on me for more. A couple of weeks ago he tells me he wants me to pony up $3 million to keep him quiet. I should have seen it coming, because he'd been acting strange. I should have had him killed then, but I thought he was bluffing. A couple of nights later, I'm sitting at home watching the news and my fax starts spitting out copies of Alpine's campaign financial records. The real ones, not the one's I was sending to Leon-Francis. I'd already destroyed the originals, but somehow Travis got his hands on some copies."

"So Travis found out you were slicing off some of Alpine's campaign contributions for yourself." Doc stood very still, trying to think as he listened.

"Yeah, but that was peanuts compared to what I was actually raking in. He called me the same night, telling me he'd talked to a reporter. He said he was going to tell her more if I didn't pay. I had no other choice but to stop her. I figured that killing Mateo would scare him into keeping his mouth shut long enough for me to find out how much he knew and where he was getting his information. I can't believe he found this place or my key. I'd give my right arm to find out how he did it."

"You've gone to a lot of expense to keep this room a secret from everyone. And that computer server over there is doing more than keeping track of your dirty money. What else are you up to?"

"You *are* clever." Shaw smiled. "You want to see?"

Doc hated fanning his ego, but he was too curious. "Only if you have the time."

Moving back to the platform, Shaw inserted an electronic key in the slotted groove on the console. The computer monitors lit up.

Doc looked up at the nearest monitor. A portfolio of stocks

and bonds filled the screen. He stepped closer to have a better look. Then he turned to the next monitor, which displayed the banking transactions for Edmund Lawrence. Shaw grinned when he saw the surprised look on Doc's face. "You're tapped into the Excalibur Group's computer network?"

"Yes! And it's totally transparent and undetectable."

"You're stealing money from Devin Leon-Francis's company and dumping it in a phony account in a Bahamian bank, and you actually think it's going to work?"

"It is working. Edmund Lawrence is just one of several aliases Leon-Francis uses. He buries his money in secret accounts, which he tracks through Excalibur's computer system. He's shuttling his assets around in so many investments and banks, he has no idea how much he has. With a creative yet simple computer algorithm I developed, I found a way to attach a modest quarter of a percent transaction fee to randomly selected accounts, the proceeds of which are deposited into my offshore bank under Edmund Lawrence. And Leon-Francis doesn't have a clue what I'm doing."

Doc thought the man must be mad. "Travis discovered what you were doing and had proof."

"So what, I don't care about any incriminating files."

"You should. I'm willing to bet your future, which is looking pretty bleak about now, that Travis uploaded copies of your transactions to Excalibur's computer system for safekeeping. It's only a matter of time before Leon-Francis finds the records and sees what you've been up to. If I'm right, he's going to be more than just a little ticked off. You know, you really are an idiot. I wouldn't make any long-range plans if I were you."

"I don't give a damn about Leon-Francis. I'm tired of hearing about him. If it weren't for me, Victor Alpine would be rotting away somewhere in a nursing home. It was me who put him where he is today. Nobody else could have done it, including that pious Devin

Leon-Francis. I was the strategist, I made people believe in him, and I'm the one who created the machine that got him here!" he shouted. The more he raged on, the more agitated he became—and the more he waved his gun at Doc. He was out of control and dangerously close to pulling the trigger.

"So, why did you end up working for a man like Leon-Francis?" The question achieved its intended purpose.

Shaw calmed down and leaned against the computer console. "Money, what else. It sure wasn't because I thought he'd actually get one of his idiots into the White House. Alpine isn't the only puppet Leon-Francis has in training. There have been at least a half-dozen over the years, but Alpine has come the closest. Leon-Francis hires people like me to get people like Alpine elected. He thinks he's God, but that's about to change."

"You actually think you're going to walk out of here a free and rich man?"

"Free and *very* rich, but nothing like what I'm about to take. Leon-Francis has built his reputation and power on his money, and I've found a way to take it all from him. I'll be drinking Tequilas in the Caribbean before he knows what hit his wrinkled ass."

Doc stared at him in disbelief. "He must have scraped the bottom of the gene pool to come up with you. It's amazing to me that you managed to survive this long."

At that moment, Kilgor emerged from the stairs that were hidden behind the computer server, pointing his gun at Shaw. "I knew we couldn't trust you! You've been lying to us all along."

Time froze for a second, then Shaw turned his gun. The men fired at the same time, but both missed.

Doc had been waiting for just such an opportunity. Quick as lightning he delivered a scissors kick to the side of Shaw's head, sending him reeling headfirst into the server. Kilgor turned his gun toward Doc, but then felt a cool barrel pressed against the back of his own skull.

Marcus squeezed the trigger. "That's for Sydney."

In the confusion that followed, Shaw disappeared down the stairs. Doc picked up Kilgor's gun and went after him. Marcus paused to kick Kilgor's corpse. A few seconds later someone slugged him over the head and he fell, unconscious.

Doc moved as fast as he could down the narrow staircase, but the lighting was poor and he couldn't see where he was going. When he reached the bottom, he found two exit doors. He picked the wrong one and couldn't get back into the building. He ran around the corner just in time to see Shaw running to his car. He was forty yards ahead of Doc, and there was no way he was going to be caught. Doc stopped, aimed, and fired. The bullet hit Shaw in the small of the back. He gasped and stumbled, falling against the car door. Somehow he managed to get in and turn on the ignition.

The Lexus exploded in a ball of flame. Pieces of Shaw's duster floated aimlessly back to the ground.

●　　●　　●

Quietly, Morgan slipped away and returned to the waiting car.

"Are they out?" Woodberry asked.

"Yeah."

Woodberry nodded. He loaded a rocket into the launcher, aimed, and fired. The projectile whistled through a window and exploded. The top floor of the warehouse collapsed--along with the rest of the building--into the bay. He handed the rocket launcher back to Morgan, who dropped it over the side of the pier into the water.

"Let's get out of here." The car drove slowly out the gate and headed north toward the airport.

Five minutes later, the police arrived and found Marcus and Sydney lying on the pier.

CHAPTER

The atrium of the Evergreen Hospital was filled with assorted Pacific Northwest perennials and indigenous evergreens, which reminded Asha of St. Croix. She watched anxiously for Doc to come through the swinging doors.

"You must be sick of this place by now. I sure am," Caitlin said.

"You would think eleven days of interrogation would be enough for the police. How much more information do they need?"

Marcus returned to the table with some soft drinks. "The doctor says Sydney can go home in about another week, but she'll need a wheelchair for a while and a lot of rest."

Caitlin reached over and gave Marcus a long kiss.

"What was that for?" he asked, wrapping his arm around her waist.

"You and Doc were lucky, too. I'm just glad you made it back in one piece. I am especially thankful to the person who saved you and Sydney."

Marcus rubbed the lump that was still noticeable on the back of his head. "Yeah, I'd like to thank the creep, too."

The doors opened, but it wasn't Doc. Asha sank back in the chair. "When is Julian coming?"

"He's still jabbering away with Sydney. I think he's trying to entice her to go into business with him. He claims I don't pay her enough to take the abuse," he said, laughing.

Asha smiled and then grimaced. She removed her sunglasses, dabbed water from her injured eye, and then replaced the glasses.

"You okay?" Marcus asked, concerned.

Even now, 3,000 miles away from home she didn't feel entirely safe from Maurice Beale. He may not have succeeded in killing her, but the fear he instilled would remain for a long time. "I'm fine, just a little sore." She spoke softly, as though her head ached.

"Anything new about Maurice?" Marcus asked.

"No, he's disappeared. As long as I never see him again, I don't care where he's gone."

"I don't think you have to worry about that. He'd be crazy to come after you again," Caitlin said.

Asha bit her lip. "He *is* crazy."

"Not crazy enough to want to take on Doc. I can guarantee you he won't be going back there again," Marcus said.

"I'm just happy to be alive and thankful that Julian is okay."

"There was never any question that he wouldn't be. The boy must have Teflon angels protecting him. You would have been proud of him Asha, he--"

"Marcus," Caitlin interrupted.

"What, what's wrong?"

"I don't think Asha is in the mood to hear any specifics."

Asha shook her head. I just want to be free of this place. Do you know when the police are going to let us go home?"

"They're through with us, at least for now. I think they finally got it through their thick skulls that we didn't make this stuff up. The authorities are going to have their hands full trying to sort out the mess. They'll be indicting half the people in Evergreen before this thing's over," Marcus said.

Caitlin hesitated. "How about Leon-Francis, are they going to arrest him?"

"Not in our lifetime," Marcus said scornfully. "They don't have anything on him. Desmond Shaw is dead, Victor Alpine is missing, and all traces of Leon-Francis's involvement went up in smoke when that missile took out the warehouse. Trust me; they stand a better chance of finding Jimmy Hoffa's body."

Asha was curious. "Any leads on what happened to Victor Alpine?"

"Nope. He vanished into thin air. The police found his wallet and glasses on his office desk. They'll never find him. He's probably wearing a cement jacket at the bottom of the bay somewhere."

Asha jumped from her chair when she saw Doc coming toward here.

"Is everything all right?" he asked.

"Yes, I just missed you," she said, nuzzling her head on his chest. "What took you so long?

He smiled and kissed her. "I just wanted to say goodbye to Sydney before we left."

"The police are letting you go?"

"Yeah, we fly out in an hour."

Asha went over to say goodbye to Caitlin.

Marcus walked over to his friend. "You two cutting out?"

"Yeah, man, it's time to leave," Doc said.

Marcus pulled him aside. "Why don't you and Asha spend a few days with us? We could both use the rest, and maybe I can convince you to join me in the business. You and I work well together."

Doc laughed. "Quik, working with you can be deadly. No thanks, but I appreciate the offer. I've got a life in the Islands and I'm anxious to get back to it. Besides, I'm trying to live a calmer life."

"Are you going to try and get your teaching job back?"

"I don't think so. I've got a few ideas in mind, but nothing definite. I'm going to lay low for a while, talk some things over with Asha, and take things from there."

"Well, I can have Peri fly you guys home."

"Thanks, but I've got it covered. We're flying down to Cancun for awhile; Asha could use the change of scenery."

She smiled as he tightened his arm around her.

"Damn, Doc. Why are you so hard? I'm trying to thank you for saving my ass. If it weren't for you, Caitlin would be a widow."

"And if you hadn't shot Kilgor, I'd be dead, and if Sydney hadn't bailed us both out, we wouldn't be having this conversation. You don't owe me anything, Quik. We're friends—always will be." The men hugged each other.

"You know, man, if you need me, I'm there," Marcus assured him. "If you ever decide to go after Maurice Beale, I'll be on the next thing smoking."

Doc's right eye twitched at the mention of Beale's name. He would stay with Asha long as it took for her to recover. But after that…there wouldn't be any place Beale could hide from him. "I know you will, but your responsibility is to your family. I can take care of my own business."

"You're going after him, aren't you?"

Doc looked grim. "What do you think?"

Marcus smirked. "Yeah, I suppose you are. That's the one thing you and I have in common. We can't leave shit unsettled. You know we also have some unfinished business with Mr. Leon-Francis."

"You're crazy."

Marcus broke out in a broad smile. "Yeah. I may be crazy, but I'm not stupid. If he don't start nuthin', won't be nuthin'."

EPILOGUE

(Two Months Later)

A white Porsche sped down the winding canyon road and turned into the security gate. The driver smiled to the guards as the car raced past, continuing its journey through 220 acres of lush green orchards sprinkled with tangelos, oranges, and tangerines. Workers recognized the owner's Porsche as it came to a stop at the end of the road, next to the log house and helipad holding a white helicopter. The house, which had been built by the movie mogul, Basham Stillwater, in 1930 as a summer retreat, was cloaked and protected by the enormous San Andreas Mountains. The house was now owned by his granddaughter and was a haven and sanctuary for his son, Devin Leon-Francis.

She opened the wide double doors leading to her master bedroom. Carla, the maid, greeted her as she entered.

"Senorita, it is nice to have you home again. I have prepared your room for you."

"Thank you, Carla. Where's my father?"

"In the study waiting for you."

Devin Leon-Francis was talking on the telephone when she entered the room. Even sitting down, he looked intimidating; his six-foot-six frame smothered the chair. She liked his new white crewcut.

"My prodigal daughter has returned," he said, hanging up the phone and moving toward her.

Sydney hugged her father tightly. He stroked her hair and kissed her. "I'm glad you're home," he whispered.

"It's so good to see you again, Dad. I missed you."

"I know. I missed you, too. It pained me that I couldn't come see you in the hospital, but I knew you would understand."

Sydney placed her finger on his lips. "Of course—it's okay. The important thing is I'm better now and we can spend the holidays together."

He gave her that all-too-familiar look, and she sighed. "When do you have to leave?"

"Tonight. A short business trip, but I'll stay in touch."

Sydney knew what that meant. It would be months before they saw each other again.

She hugged him. "I'm grateful we can at least spend Thanksgiving together."

"What excuse did you give St. John for leaving?"

"That I needed some time away."

"Then you haven't told him yet about running off to the Virgin Islands with Sebasst?"

Sydney raised her head from her father's chest. "How did you know that?"

"I make it my business to know what other people are doing, especially my daughter. I can't believe you're contemplating going into business with him."

"I'm a bodyguard, Dad. That's what I do. Julian knows a lot of people in Washington D.C. who will be happy to pay for our services."

"I don't like it, and I know your mother wouldn't either, if she were alive." He walked over to the large painting of Angela Belleshota hanging on the wall. "I am just amazed how much you look like her. You inherited her beauty and, unfortunately, her independent spirit."

He turned to face his daughter. "I just don't know why you can't do something normal with your life instead of risking it for other people who don't give a damn about you."

Sydney sat in her father's chair. "My life is my own, Dad. I make my own choices, and I'm perfectly capable of taking care of myself."

"You call getting shot up and almost dying taking care of yourself?"

"But I didn't die."

"Only because my boys saved you and St. John at St. John's place *and* in that warehouse."

"We could have handled it. How did you know they were coming after us?"

"Shaw called Jason Worrick with some silly-ass story about St. John wanting my head because he blamed me for the death of his friend. Of course, the fool didn't know you were my daughter, or that I knew he was stealing from me. I just didn't know how he was doing it. I'll give him credit; he was clever. He was hoping I'd kill St. John and the worthless little band of mercenaries he was paying for with *my* money. I must be slipping in my old age, because I used to be a better judge of character."

"What did you do with Victor Alpine?"

"I haven't seen Victor, and as long as he doesn't talk or show his face in public again, he doesn't have to worry about me."

Sydney stared at the floor. "Why did you do it, dad? Don't you already have enough?"

Leon-Francis looked at his lovely daughter. She would never understand the compulsive addiction for power. The more you have, the more you want. "I can't be president of the United States. I'd at least like to own one before I die," he joked.

Sydney didn't laugh. She knew she would never know the truth. Her father was the most evasive person she knew, but that's why he had survived so long. "I know we've always been open and honest in our relationship with each other. You don't care for the work I do and

I certainly don't like what you do. But you're my father, and I'll always love you—no matter what you've done. I want you to be truthful with me. Did you have anything to do with Julian's sister's death?"

"Sydney, I'm not proud of most of the things I've done in this life, and I suppose that will work itself out on Judgment Day. But the one thing I hold very dear to me is your respect. That's why I've never lied to you and never will. I never sanctioned a hit on Eva Ward or, for that matter, Anna Mateo. And I certainly didn't give Shaw authority to do it."

"Do you know a man named Maurice Beale?"

"Never heard of him. Who is he?"

"Oh, never mind. It's not important." She rose from the chair and kissed her father on the cheek.

"Good, because I'm starving. Let's go see if that turkey of Carla's is ready."

* * *

After dinner, Leon-Francis placed a call to his secretary. "Jason, we need to tie up another loose end. Have Woodberry and Morgan find Beale. Tell them to give him the same retirement plan they gave Victor Alpine."

CHASING THE STORM

(An Excerpt)

By Dwight M. Edwards

Jordan waited until evening before setting out from the village on her journey. A red-footed falcon followed her snowmobile as it streaked across the snow-covered mesa. Wild reindeer and wolves sought refuge from the heavy snow and wind that pounded the mountain. It was midnight by the time she reached the summit, but light as day, thanks to the northern lights showering the heavens with their kaleidoscopic colors.

The bird watched as she struggled through the inhospitable sanctuary of frozen tundra and dangerous glaciers. Wind-blown snow covered the tracks of the snowmobile as it disappeared into the forest. Jordan, dressed in a white snowsuit, Tossu overboots and a facemask, worked quickly in the subzero temperature. She hid the snowmobile under a white tarp and made sure her equipment was secure before trudging off through the thigh-deep snow.

It took her an hour to reach the edge of a wide precipice overlooking the canyon. The bottom of the canyon was as flat as a plate, due to sediment deposits from an ancient river that once flowed through the mountain. She checked her coordinates to make sure she had the right location. This was the place. She scanned the grounds with electronic binoculars. There were eight acres of pristine snow and woods below, marred only by a series of intersecting ski tracks circling the perimeter grounds. Two guards patrolled the woods directly below her, and another one stood on the road leading to the house chiseled in the side of the mountain. A white Apache helicopter sat on a twelve-foot high platform next to the house.

The snowstorm was getting worse and the temperature was dropping. Most of the guards abandoned their posts for the warmth of the inside. Jordan dusted the snow from her lens and stuffed the binoculars back into her pack. It was time to go.

The falcon watched her rappel down the side of the canyon wall and cross an ice bridge, before dropping down to the ground. She removed her backpack and set up a position 800 meters from the house. She dug a shelter pit to wait for the storm to pass. It didn't.

By 2:00 a raging blizzard howled though the canyon, forcing all but one man indoors. The lone guard stood on the road with his back against the wind and his hands wrapped around a cup of hot coffee. Jordan could not afford to wait any longer. She slithered down the bank and crawled along the ravine to the concrete culvert that supported the road, where she attached the explosives.

● ● ●

Devin Leon-Francis laid two more logs in the mammoth fireplace that was sandwiched between the floor-to-ceiling bookcases. He jabbed at the burning wood until the fire exploded into flames, shooting hot embers up in the belly of the mountain. Resting the poker against the fireplace, he stood up and straightened the crooked oil painting hanging over the mantel.

Jason Worrick was lying on the sofa in front of the window. "This damn weather is going to keep me up all night." He squirmed under the covers, trying to get his naked legs warmed by the fire.

Leon-Francis stood at the mirror, adjusting his tie and playing with his thick, perfectly coifed silver hair. He had a square-jawed face with a mustache that covered his thin lips. Bony fingers were the only things that gave away his true age. "I have to go," he said.

"You're going out in this weather?" Worrick asked.

"Yes."

Worrick sat upright on the couch. "You coming back?"

"I'll send for you in a couple of weeks or so, after my business is finished. I need you to stay here and wrap things up."

Worrick flinched as a burst of pain shot through his hipbone and down his legs. Leon-Francis watched the old man's wrinkled hand squeezing the edge of the couch in pain, but he didn't move to help. He passed Worrick the handkerchief from his breast pocket.

"Thanks," Worrick said, wiping his mouth. "You must have a hot date to risk your life going out in this weather."

"I do. With Sasha Micheaux."

"It's horrible out there . . . you sure this can't wait until morning?"

"The secret in the art of war lies in an eye for locality and not letting the right moment slip through your fingertips. Now is the right time."

"Whatever Chinese philosopher said that never met the Micheauxs or the other Merovingians."

Leon-Francis stroked the fire again, "Superior force never guarantees victory, Jason, especially if you don't know what to defend against. Sasha will soon discover that."

"You think you can knock off the queen bee without the Merovingians getting upset?"

"The other families won't interfere."

Worrick wanted to ask him how he knew that, but he had learned from thirty-five years of working with his boss not to ask certain questions, and this was one.

Leon-Francis survived by two principles: never tell anyone more than they need to know; and never trust anyone. He had an intelligence network superior to most third world countries, and always stayed a step ahead of his adversaries.

Jason Worrick was Leon-Francis' only friend and second in command, but like everyone else who worked for Devin Leon-Francis—Worrick was also kept in the dark about most things. Leon-Francis shuffled his personnel like pawns on a chessboard, in a game where only he knew the outcome.

"You've got Sasha's brothers out of the way, and now you have the media and authorities breathing down her neck. Let them finish her off . . . why take extra risk?" Worrick asked.

"I am going to finish what I started. The Micheauxs had their chances to do business with me."

"So why do I have to stay here?"

"I need for you to take over the operation in Narvik until I find a replacement for Andy Preston."

"Why—what's wrong with Andy?"

"He's a drunk and he's chasing some skirt all around Europe. I don't need him anymore. He's out."

"He's still a kid, Devin. He's homesick, maybe a little love struck, but harmless."

Leon-Francis gave him a cool stare. "He knows too much about . . . this place . . . and my daughter. Woodberry will talk with him." He put on his overcoat and gloves. Worrick sighed as he rested his arms on his cane. Leon-Francis lightly brushed his hand across his felt hat. "You're taking this too personal, Jason."

"The kid was beginning to grow on me, that's all."

Leon-Francis smiled. "What's the update on my daughter?"

"She and St. John are still in Switzerland trying to get an audience with her Royal Highness, Sasha Micheaux."

"They're wasting their time."

"Tell that to St. John. That guy doesn't know when to quit. He's never going to give up searching for us. All he needs is a sniff and he will be all over my butt. I've been hiding up here for six weeks, ever since we put your plan into operation. This is getting ridiculous. Why do you insist on keeping that fool alive? He's dangerous." Worrick used his cane and tried lifting himself off the sofa. "This damn weather isn't good for my rheumatoid arthritis. You need to get me out of here to someplace warm . . . anyplace other than this frozen wasteland."

Leon-Francis helped him to his feet. "St. John is nothing without Julian Sebasst—and he's being taken care of as we speak. You're safe here. In a few weeks this will all be over and I'll send you back home, but right now there . . ."

A bullet shattered the triangular window next to them, spraying the room with glass shrapnel. A second shot barely missed Leon-Francis's head and blew a chunk of granite from the wall. Leon-Francis fell to the floor. He opened his eyes and saw a golf ball-size hole in Worrick's neck. Pandemonium broke out as armed men swarmed from the house. There was another unheard shot, and a guard fell face down in the snow. Two more shots and more men fell. The guards fired their weapons into the empty forest until the whole canyon sounded like an erupting volcano.

Two guards found an abandoned sniper rifle lying next to one of their dead men. They followed the tracks for forty yards, before realizing the shooter had circled behind them. The noise from Jordan's shotgun blasts alerted the others. Five yellow snowmobiles shot from underneath the helicopter platform, followed by men on skies. They made it halfway across the road, before an explosion ripped the culvert apart, sending men and machines flying.

Jordan watched the carnage from the ridge—her finger still glued to the trigger on the detonator. She took one last look down at the burning men before tossing the detonator in the snow, and continuing up the ridge.

It took her two hours to reach the foot of Nehemiah's Wall, and fifteen minutes to dig out the provisions and gear she had buried. She chewed her rations while changing out of her wet clothes. Jordan slipped on new thermal underwear, an Icelandic sweater, and a new snowsuit. The facemask was discarded for a ski cap and goggles. She shoved her service revolver in her holster, tested the tether line securing the skis to the backpack, and made sure her boot crampons were on tight. Jordan looked at the immense wall of ice staring her in the face. Getting over the wall was the easy part. Getting to Fauske where her boat was waiting to take her home was going to be a lot more difficult now. The weather was getting worse, she still had miles to go to cross the mountain and glaciers, and Leon-Francis's men would likely be waiting for her in Fauske. She took two deep breaths, swung her axe deep into the ice, and lifted herself up on the 810-foot icefall.

* * *

A white-headed man they called the Norwegian led his patrol up the mountain where they spent two hours hunting for Jordan on the summit. All they found was her snowmobile. As they returned to camp, the Norwegian passed a row of dead bodies' spaced neatly apart covered in snow. The section of road that once covered the culvert was now a giant hole and repository of body parts. The Norwegian picked up a severed hand by his foot and threw it in the hole with the other parts. He looked for Woodberry. He found him standing in the riverbed with his hands in his pocket, barking out orders. Woodberry not only looked like a marine drill sergeant, he was as tough as one. The Norwegian knew it would be a long night.

Tiberius Woodberry inspected Jordan's snowmobile from the riverbed. "Where did you find it?"

"Up on the summit, a couple of kilometers from here," the Norwegian said.

"Which direction is he headed?"

"We didn't find any tracks."

"That doesn't make sense." The Norwegian grabbed Woodberry's hand and helped him up the slippery bank. "Put the snowmobile in the shed . . . I'll check it later." He grabbed the Norwegian by the shoulder as he was leaving. "And then I want you to send two more patrols back up to the summit and find me something . . . a body, a turd, something that tells me which way he went. You came highly recommended, let's see you earn your money."

The Norwegian nodded his head.

Woodberry headed back to the house. "Get these men out of here and bury them!" he said, passing the corpses and slamming the door behind him. The fire in the fireplace was out and men were nailing cedar planks over the shattered windows to keep the snow out. Jason Worrick's body was stretched out on the sofa under a blood-soaked blanket covered in snow. Woodberry ran up the steps to the loft and went down the hall to the master bedroom.

Devin Leon-Francis sat in his easy chair, reading. "I know you have some good news for me," he said, without moving his eyes from the book.

"There was only one shooter. We found his snowmobile on the top. He won't get far on foot in this weather."

"Why aren't you holding his ass in your hands?"

Woodberry shifted uncomfortably on his feet. "I don't . . . have his ass yet, sir, but I will. My guess is he is heading to Fauske . . . that's the nearest town from here."

Leon-Francis lowered the book from his face. "Let me see if I understand you so far," he said, tossing the paperback into the open suitcase on the bed. "Some maniac rolled up here, to my home that no one is supposed to even know exists . . . kills Jason . . . my boys, and you can't find him. Does that about size up the situation?"

"I believe we're dealing with a professional. The rifle we found was a British . . ."

Leon-Francis jumped to his feet. His voice was soft—almost a whisper, but his gun-metal eyes were red. "I don't care about belief, Tiberius, I only deal in fact. Let me give you the facts we're currently dealing with. First, your boys didn't do their jobs. Second, someone in this organization opened his mouth about this place. Third, I don't like people trying to kill me." He inched closer to his face. "I want this man, and I want you to get him now. There are only two ways off this mountain—across the summit and over Nehemiah's Wall. I want your boys waiting for him when he comes down the other side. Are we clear on this?"

"Sir, the road is destroyed. How are . . ."

"High jump over, or bungee across . . . it doesn't matter to me. Get him, and then I want you to go to Narvik and find out who Andy Preston has been running his big mouth to."

"Yes, sir."

Leon-Francis closed his suitcase. "I'm leaving. I'll get back to you and you better have some good news for me. Don't let me down again, Tiberius."

Leon-Francis walked through the tunnel leading to the helicopter platform. The helicopter lifted off the pad and hovered above the fortress that he knew he would never see again. "Get me out of here," he yelled to his pilot.

●　●　●

The anticipated storm hit the Norwegian coastline with hurricane force. The French freighter, *Vincien Micheaux,* sat disabled, bobbling helplessly back and forth in the blue waters of jagged ice. The French captain checked the ship's position again and took another look through the binoculars. He was searching for the tugboats, but he only saw the heavy fog and freezing rain that engulfed the pilothouse window. He was beginning to regret having destroyed the communications and radar equipment, but it was better to be safe than sorry. Two of the imprisoned crew had escaped and tried to radio for help before they were caught by his men. He didn't want to take any chances that something else could go wrong so he had the equipment smashed and tossed overboard. That was before the storm set in and twenty-foot swells pushed the ship off course. The captain had no idea of where they were, but he knew they couldn't survive the night in this weather. Suddenly, he heard a faint whistle off in the distance. He pointed the floodlights toward the sound. "There!" he shouted in French to his five deckhands waiting below. "Off starboard."

The captain blew the freighter's whistle once and then twice more. The first tugboat came into view and moved astern, followed by a second tug. Off the portside bow, appeared a third tugboat, but it dwarfed the other two. It was a huge yellow 300-foot salvage tug with a floating crane, divers, and a crew of eighteen men dressed in red-clad Columbia raincoats. They jumped off the boats and secured the lines to the freighter.

Floodlights burned as the men transferred the cargo from the freighter onto the tugboats. Men in red wet suits worked underwater securing the explosives to the hull and propeller shaft of the freighter. After they finished their work, they waited for the boss. An hour later, a white helicopter landed on top of the salvage tug.

The French captain hustled up the platform steps to get what he thought was going to be his final instructions from Devin Leon-Francis. Instead, Leon-Francis' men shot the captain and his deckhands and threw their bodies overboard. Ten minutes later, Leon-Francis and his helicopter were gone.

Leon-Francis' men cast off the lines and two of the tugboats disappeared back into the fog, leaving the wounded freighter at the mercy of the salvage tug. The tug pushed the larger vessel 144 miles north of the Arctic Circle, and detonated the explosives. The *Vincien Micheaux* sank to the bottom of the Barents Sea, along with thirty-one of Sasha Micheaux's personal bodyguards locked in the cargo hold.